# TAKER OF SKULLS

## BOOK FIVE OF THE KORMAK SAGA

## WILLIAM KING

Typhon Press Limited
GLASGOW, SCOTLAND

\* \* \*

MORE BOOKS BY WILLIAM KING

Stealer of Flesh

Defiler of Tombs

Weaver of Shadow

City of Strife

Taker of Skulls

Ocean of Fear

Born of Darkness

Sword of Wrath

Masque of Death

# CHAPTER ONE

KORMAK RODE DOWN the steep trail into Varigston, ready to put spurs to his pony or hand to his blade. Here on the disputed border between Aquilea and Taurea his grey-flecked black hair and tall, rangy frame marked him as no Taurean. All it would take would be for one of the Sunlanders to decide he was the scout for a raiding party and he would be facing a lynch mob or summary execution. The closer you got to Aquilean territory, the more suspicious the gold-hair colonists became. And they had reason—the Aquilean hill men deserved their reputation as savage slayers of all who invaded what they considered as their land.

A cold wind blew off the peaks and there was a trace of sleet even though it was early autumn in the lowlands. In the mountains, winter extended its talons early. The chill breeze brought back half-buried memories of Kormak's childhood in Aquilea. He had lived in that bleak land until he was eight years old.

He was still in Taurean-controlled territory—he could tell by the league-posts that counted the distance to the capital and the occasional patrols of knights and their men-at-arms he had met on his way. Those hard-bitten men had told tales of goblins in the hills and other stranger things; of giant vampire bats swarming through the night and monsters stalking the hillsides.

He was glad of that. Their reports gave him an excuse for being in the area that no one would question. His instructions had come under the red seal direct from the Grandmaster of the Order of the Dawn, coded most urgent and most secret.

He was curious about that. Normally, such dispatches concerned the clandestine assassination of some powerful nobleman or influential cleric. This time the terse message had told him only to get to Varigston as quickly as possible. He was to remain at the sign of the Axe and Hammer until he received further instructions. That, too, told him something about the mission. The Grandmaster feared to put down anything more.

His pony carried him down the rocky path into the edge of the town. It was a mixture of thatched drystane-built cottages and newer wooden structures. All of the timber buildings had a shabby, gaudy look. Even on the newest structures the bright paint was peeling as the mountain weather ate away at the tawdry finery. Varigston had not looked like this the last time he had passed this way but that had been two decades ago. Then it had been a drab place of sheep farmers and a few would-be miners prospecting for silver in the nearby mountains.

None of the hedge-knights he had met en route had a good word to say about the town. They claimed that anyone who lived there was beyond the pale, and looking at the place Kormak could understand why. In the past few years the business of looting a long dead and supposedly haunted ancient city had turned a sleepy village on the north-eastern border of Taurea into a desperate boom-town. The finding of Khazduroth had brought a new prosperity and a ferocious energy to Varigston. Kormak was not sure this was an improvement.

If he had not known better he would have sworn the place was a bandits' lair. There were too many armed men for a community of its size and not enough farmers, shepherds or peasants. On his way up, he had encountered some of the merchants who shipped grain and ale and dried meat in, and took away all sorts of stuff in return. There were people down in less wild lands that would pay good money for the dwarf artefacts found in Khazduroth.

The main street ran through the lowest part of a long valley and was lined with taverns and brothels and shops selling everything that prospectors could need, and lots of things they did not.

Priests of the Holy Sun offered blessings. Some of them were mendicant holy men. Some of them were imposters. Beggars stretched out their hands and implored a copper piece. Shady characters tried to sell him maps guaranteed to lead to a lode of treasure amid the ruins of the lost city, and cursed his departing back when he showed no interest. Rough looking bravoes studied him carefully, took note of his size and manner and well-worn gear and came to the conclusion it was not worth trying to intimidate him or rob him. Women studied him through the open windows of bawdy houses. They wore no tops and in the cold their nipples stood erect, which he supposed was the point.

Despite his earlier fears, no one paid him too much attention and he understood why. There were Aquilean hill men here aplenty, come to trade and drink, looking around with barely concealed wonder at what was, no doubt, the biggest town they had ever entered without their swords in their hands and blue war-paint on their faces.

The streets were filled with horses and ponies and mules and wagons and a bustle of people. For a town at the far end of nowhere Varigston was a busy place. Kormak drew his steed to a halt as a drunk was ejected through the doors of a tavern by a massive bouncer. He picked himself up, shook his fist and then limped away.

Overhead the massive peaks loomed, mocking all the human activity into insignificance. Grey clouds obscured their snow-clad tops and swirled in the sky in a way that he remembered well from his childhood.

His destination was the best looking tavern in town. Over the door hung a signboard depicting two crossed dwarvish weapons, an axe and a hammer. There was an inscription in what was meant to look like dwarven script but it was gibberish. Kormak doubted than many of the customers would be able to tell though. Very few people indeed could read that ancient tongue. Kormak knew dwarvish was really just a variant of the Old Tongue with its own runic script but whoever had made the sign had not. The lettering meant nothing.

He tied his mount to the rail then walked through the swinging doors. The smell of beer and tobacco and dreamsmoke assaulted his nostrils. The clamour of men drunk in the late afternoon fell upon his ears and then ceased.

The silence lengthened as everyone turned to stare at him. He stood in the doorway and glanced around, meeting the gaze of anyone who looked at him, taking in the full details of the common room as he did so.

The walls were old, and built of mountain stone and the bar looked heavy and ancient, but there were tapestries from Vermstadt and the trading cities of western Belaria hung over them. Some gaudy murals were on the ceiling, showing fanciful portraits of dwarves and heroic prospectors. The new stuff spoke of a lot of wealth gained quickly and splashed onto the walls to attract a certain clientele.

A massive man with a scarred, skeletal face stared at him. A good-looking woman sat with him. She adjusted the round glasses perched on the bridge of her nose and the fingers of her left hand flickered through a complex gesture of greeting.

He felt a shock of recognition. He had last seen this woman more than twenty years ago and she did not appear to have aged a day. Given what Kormak knew her to be, that was hardly surprising, but some of the ways that she could have achieved that ageless look would stain her soul black.

As he strode over towards them, a drunk stumbled against him. Kormak grabbed the drunk's hand and snapped the fingers that fumbled for his purse. The man screamed and ran for the door, suddenly no longer quite so drunk but in considerably more pain. No one else tried to stop Kormak before he reached the booth.

"Mind if I join you?" he said. The man looked at the woman as if for instructions. He was big as Kormak. His head was shaved and a nasty scar marked his right cheek, cut all the way down to the jaw. She gestured at the table. "Be my guest."

"You're a long way from home, Lady Karnea" Kormak said. "The last I heard you were dwelling in Belaria."

The woman had rosy cheeks and sparkling blue eyes. Her nose was small. Her honey-blonde hair was tied in a single braid bound by a clip of blue stone worked with what looked like an authentic dwarvish rune.

"At the Forlorn Tower, in the Silver Mountains," she said.

"I see you retain your interest in dwarves." Kormak spoke quietly. He glanced around. No one seemed to be paying them much attention, but you never knew.

The woman smiled. It transformed her face. Where before she had been merely pretty, now she was lovely. "I do indeed. It is good to see you again, Kormak," she said. "I was told we would meet you here, if all went well."

"Who told you that?"

"A mutual acquaintance."

"You carry an interesting blade," said the man, much more quietly. His voice had a hoarseness to it, as if he had spent too much time shouting orders on a battlefield. "Dwarf-forged, by the look of it."

"Indeed, Boreas," said the woman. "Look at the hilt. It is quite clearly Khazduri workmanship. A Stentarian era original, overlaid with late-Gromani fretwork unless I am much mistaken."

The lovely smile widened. "As you surmised, I am still a scholar of the Khazduri," the woman said. "That is why I am here."

"Go on," Kormak said. He doubted that this meeting was a coincidence. He had last seen this woman at Mount Aethelas. It seemed likely she was his contact. If she wasn't, he still wanted to find out why someone like her was here.

Karnea removed her glasses, breathed on the lenses, polished them, held them up to the light and inspected them and then put them back on her nose. "There are things we need to talk about and Boreas tells me this is not the right place to do so."

Kormak stared at her. She seemed unworldly but there was something about her, a sense of concealed power that made him edgy, that he had only been vaguely aware of when he was younger. Since then he had encountered many people like Karnea, usually when he had been sent to kill them.

"This looks like a tough place," Kormak said. He kept his voice neutral.

"Does it? Boreas keeps telling me so but so far the people all have seemed friendly enough to me."

"Maybe because Boreas has been with you," Kormak said.

"We have a private chamber above," said Boreas. "It is in the corner of the house, the walls are thick and there is little chance we will be overheard. Perhaps we should retire there before we discuss anything further?"

"After you," Kormak said. Boreas did not look like a man he wanted behind him in a dark corner of an inn. It did not matter to Kormak whether these were the people who the Grandmaster had sent him to meet. He had not lived as long as he had by taking unnecessary chances.

The skull-faced man gave him a sour grin as if he understood exactly what Kormak was thinking. He lifted a heavy warhammer from beside the table and led the way up the stairs, Karnea trailing behind him.

Kormak followed, wondering what all this was about, and whether he was walking into a trap.

# CHAPTER TWO

THE WALLS OF this inn were old and thick. Their room was at the far end of a dark corridor. Kormak moved cautiously, holding himself in readiness in case anyone leapt out from the shadowy alcoves or doorways.

They reached the last room at the back of the inn, and when they did so, Karnea looked around to make sure they were unobserved and then muttered something. The brief flash of heat Kormak felt from the Elder Sign on his chest confirmed the woman was using magic.

"Nothing has been disturbed," she said. Boreas produced a key, opened the door and stepped through. Karnea followed him. Kormak went in last and made sure he stepped to one side, keeping his back to the wall as he did so.

"You are a cautious one," said Boreas.

"It has kept me alive," Kormak said.

Karnea's glance passed between the two of them. She suddenly understood she was in a situation where violent death might swiftly ensue, if the wrong thing was said or done. "With your permission, Sir Kormak, Boreas will lock the door and I shall raise some wards that ensure we are not eavesdropped upon by concealed listeners... or by other means."

Kormak studied the chamber. It was large, and furnished with rough looking wooden furniture. There was a huge four-poster bed in the centre of the room and a pile of blankets thrown on the floor next to a pack that suggested Boreas slept there. At the window was a table and chair, clearly intended to be used as a desk. There was a large wardrobe in the corner which might have concealed a couple of men. He moved over to it, opened it and found nothing but clothing and stowed packs. It looked like he had only these two to deal with whatever happened.

"Go ahead," he said.

Karnea produced four rune-marked stones from her purse, placed them in each corner of the room, closed her eyes and muttered another invocation. The Elder Sign on Kormak's breast felt a little warmer as the currents of magic eddied around him.

Karnea's eyes snapped open. A look of concentration passed across her face. Boreas turned the key in the lock and dropped the bar. Kormak stood ready. If there was going to be trouble, now was when it would most likely happen.

"Good. We are secure." Karnea said. She slumped down on the bed. Her face was flushed and she sounded a little winded. Performing magic was always draining. Kormak did not lower his guard. It might be a trick, after all.

Boreas put down his hammer, leaning it against the wall beside the window. "Feel a little more relaxed now, do we?" he asked. There was a taunting edge to his words. Kormak merely smiled coldly, not allowing himself to be goaded.

"Before we go any further tell me why we are here," Kormak said.

"I have orders for you, under the red seal," Karnea said. "If I may, I will produce them."

Kormak nodded and she fumbled within the same pack from which she had produced the ward stones. Kormak held himself ready. A wizard might carry many powerful adjuncts in such a place and some of them would enable the almost instantaneous casting of magic. Karnea produced only a folded square of parchment. She moved over to hand it to Kormak. He shook his head.

"Put it on the table and then move away." She did as she was told.

Kormak removed the amulet from beneath his tunic with his left hand, walked over and touched the paper. It did not catch fire. There was no sizzling sound of a spell being disrupted. No sensation of any magic whatsoever. He returned the amulet to its place and picked up the letter. It was sealed with wax, imprinted with the blurred outlines of an old dragon sigil. There was a slight scratch on the dragon's breast. It was not impressive. It was not meant to be. It looked authentic.

Kormak opened the letter. In it was a message in a variant of the Old Tongue understood by very few these days. It said: Listen to what Lady Karnea has to say, inspect the object she bears and then do all within your power to ensure her quest's success. Keep her alive at the cost of your life if need be. He recognised the hand-writing of Grandmaster Darius.

Kormak folded the letter, tore it to shreds and threw it into the fire. He stirred the pieces with the poker, until he saw they were all consumed. His jaw tightened. It was all very well for Darius to talk about laying down his life if need be. He would not be the one doing the dying.

"It seems I am to be your bodyguard," he said. He could not keep the edge of anger from showing in his voice.

Karnea's eyes widened and she took a step back. "Is that such a terrible thing?"

"I am a Guardian of the Order of the Dawn," Kormak said. "It is my task to uphold the Law, not watch over sorcerers."

"Not all sorcerers serve the Shadow."

"In my experience those who don't usually serve themselves."

Her cheeks flushed and her eyes narrowed. She suddenly looked a lot more menacing. "Perhaps you should hear me out before you judge," she said.

"Show me this thing that the Grandmaster writes of," Kormak said. Karnea rolled up her sleeves. A metal band glittered on her forearm. It hung there loosely, as if it had been made for a larger arm and poorly adjusted to her more slender limb.

She stepped closer and held it up so he could see it. Inset in the metal was a rune. It shimmered like quicksilver.

"Notice anything unusual about it?" Karnea asked.

"It's dwarf work, of an odd sort."

"Notice anything else?" Her tone was that of a teacher disappointed in a pupil being slow of uptake. It was a tone Kormak had heard quite often during his training on Mount Aethelas, when Karnea had sometimes lectured there.

"There is something about the rune. It is similar to those on my blade."

She let out a long sigh. "It is. Have you ever seen its like before?"

He thought for a moment. "No."

She smiled at that. The dim pupil was showing some sign of intelligence after all.

"And you won't have. It is one of the Lost Runes."

"What?"

"Of the one hundred and forty four great runes, only sixty-three are currently recorded."

"Then how do you know this is one of the Lost?"

She walked over to the fire, thrust her hand into it, picked up a red hot coal. She walked over to where he stood and opened her fingers. Kormak could feel the heat radiating from the coal. Her fingers were not burned though. She showed no sign of discomfort. She tossed the coal back into the fireplace and then touched his cheek with her hand. It felt cool. Her touch was curiously intimate.

She stepped back. She opened her hands and spoke a word. A runic symbol the same as the one on her arm appeared between her fingers, written in lines of fire that slowly faded.

"This is Mankh, the Rune of Firebinding. It absorbs heat and then unleashes it at the user's command. It is a tool, a protection and a weapon. It is referred to in ancient tales but nowhere have we found a copy. Until now."

"How did you come by it?"

"It showed up nine months ago, carried to my home by a trader who had heard of my interest in dwarven relics and felt he would get a good price."

"Did he?"

"Not as much as he deserved. This is a treasure without price to students of the Khazduri."

"And that's why we are here?"

"I questioned the merchant to find out where the rune originated. The trail led here."

"You believe it came from Khazduroth?"

"He bought it from a prospector here in Varigston who found it in the deeps below Khazduroth. He told me the rune had been found by looters amid the remains of a dwarvish forge."

"Where is this merchant now?"

"On his way back to Northrock, having been told that he will get the same price if he brought me more."

"You told him what it was, of course?"

She pursed her lips, perhaps resenting the fact that he was mocking her. "Of course not."

"You did not want him suspecting the true value of what he had."

"It would be impossible to tell him the true value. Such runes have powerful magical properties—as I have just demonstrated."

"And you feel there might be more like it."

"Where one Lost Rune is found, there might be more. Khazduroth was only rediscovered just over four summers ago. Who knows what's down there?"

"You want to find out."

"What Khazduri scholar would not? But that was not all. Do you recognise the metal the rune is inlaid with?"

Kormak shook his head.

"It is an alloy of netherium." Kormak found he was holding his breath. Netherium was the metal the dwarves had taken in payment for the forging of blades like the one Kormak carried.

"That cannot be."

"I assure you it is."

"The Order scoured the world for netherium over a thousand years ago. It found none. The dwarves refused to make any more blades because the Order could not pay them."

Karnea sighed and once more he felt like a slow student. "No. They made no more blades because they could not. Netherium and its alloys are an integral component of the creation of such weapons."

Kormak understood now why the Order of the Dawn had sent him. No such blades had been forged in a thousand years. The dwarves could not even repair some of the ones that were damaged. The merchant had indeed no idea of the treasure he had sold, but then how could he? Very few had encountered the metal in the last millennium.

"You told the Grandmaster this?" Kormak said.

"I visited Mount Aethelas before I came here. I spoke with Darius."

Kormak remembered gossip from when he had been an initiate, that Karnea and the Grandmaster had been lovers back then. Of course that was before Darius had risen to the heights of power he now occupied.

"And he put me at your disposal," Kormak said. He was unable to keep the sourness from his voice. He had been pulled from protecting human beings from the powers of Shadow to aid this woman in her quest. Despite his resentment excitement grew within him. If they could find what she was looking for...

"It was not quite that way," she said. "If I could have done this without telling anyone, I would have. If word gets out, there are those who would kill to prevent such knowledge being rediscovered."

The Old Ones certainly would. And there were those who would wish to keep such lore as the Rune of Firebinding to themselves if they knew it existed. It would grant them a tremendous amount of power. Indeed the Order itself would probably take steps to secure such potent secrets. Perhaps that was why he was really here.

"So why can't you do this yourself?"

"Because there are strange monsters lurking in the depths of Khazduroth."

"You are a sorcerer, and by all accounts a powerful one, could you not guard yourself?"

"I am a scholar not a war wizard."

"So you need the aid of a man with a dwarf-forged blade."

"Darius thought it would be better to direct a single Guardian here in secret rather than send a force."

"He did not want anyone to realise the importance of your quest, you mean."

"Your grasp of the situation is sound."

"What have you done so far?"

"We have been awaiting your presence before proceeding with inquiries," she said.

"You have gold?" Kormak said.

She nodded. "Solari disks and letters of credit drawn on the Oldberg Bank in Vermstadt."

"I doubt anybody would be too interested in taking those here," Kormak said.

She gave him a sharp smile. "You might be surprised. A number of reputable merchants have representatives here. A surprisingly large amount of money passes through this place."

"The scavengers?" Kormak said.

"I believe the preferred term is prospectors," Karnea said.

"They are picking the bones of a dwarf city," Kormak said.

"It is better than letting all the treasures never see the light of day," she said. She shrugged. "If you want the truth I am pleased to join their ranks. I have long wanted to see a Khazduri city."

Kormak wondered if the woman was entirely sane. The ruins of Khazduroth were a famously dangerous place, full of ancient traps, crumbling stonework, hideous monsters, and prospectors who would cheerfully slit their own mother's throats at the prospect of profit.

Since the gates of the city had been rediscovered five years ago countless people had died there. She did not seem to find the idea of going there at all intimidating.

"Would it not be better to send someone else to find what you seek?"

She looked suddenly shifty. "It's not that I don't trust you or Boreas, Sir Kormak, far from it. But I will know what I am looking for when I see it. It would take me years to explain all the little details to you and still you might make mistakes. No, I think it best that I lead this expedition in person."

Kormak weighed her words, hearing the evasiveness in them. It might be as she said. It might be that, like many another sorcerer, she had no wish to share her secrets. Or it might just be that she was excited by the prospect of visiting Khazduroth and did not want to pass up the opportunity.

"Anyway, now that you are here, we should be about our business," Karnea said. "I must confess I am quite excited by what we might uncover. We'll need to find tools and supplies, and maybe porters and a few guards as well. A guide from among the prospectors is necessary, someone who knows their way around the Underhalls."

"That's a lot of loose lips."

"I doubt any of them will realise what we are after," Karnea said. "They will think we are just treasure hunters like themselves."

Kormak doubted that. Karnea seemed as unlikely a tomb robber as he could imagine. At best people might assume she was a rich dilettante looking for thrills. There seemed no reason to tell her this though.

"Then let's make a start," Kormak said. "We'd best find the guides first. They can tell us what we'll need by way of supplies."

# CHAPTER THREE

THAT EVENING THEY spent long hours trawling through ever sleazier taverns, climbing ever higher on the ridges above the town and closer to the outskirts. They showed Karnea's rune to people, making light of its worth yet letting them know they would be interested in finding more like it.

Those who looked like they might have the knowledge and skills required did not want to go. They had found something profitable and sold it or they would have been in the Underhalls still seeking, not down here in Varigston guzzling ale. They did not want to leave till their money was gone. The prospectors were part of a class of scavengers who wandered from dwarvish ruin to dwarvish ruin picking the places clean after they were discovered. Khazduroth was the biggest motherlode of their lifetimes.

There were others—shifty, desperate-looking men who could not answer the most basic questions Karnea put to them in a convincing manner. They wanted her money but they could not do what she wanted.

Now they were in the last and roughest looking tavern of them all. The prospectors stared at Karnea sullenly. They were a hard looking bunch, and they had been drinking, and they seemed intent on treating what Karnea was saying as a joke. There were a dozen of them, and they did not look too impressed by Boreas and Kormak. They were big men themselves, roughly dressed, wearing their hair in what they all thought was a dwarvish fashion, beards braided down to their waists and in some cases forked.

"You ever seen a rune torque like this?" Karnea was saying to their spokesman. He was half a head shorter than the largest of the prospectors but he was far broader both about the shoulder and the belly. An old rune-headed dwarf hammer lay on the table in front of him. Brown stuff and a tuft of something was stuck to one side of it. Kormak guessed the prospector was not too fussy about cleaning it.

"Nice work," he said. "And worth a pretty penny, no doubt. I've seen weapons and armour and shields. I've seen runestones and everglow lanterns and statues of the Gods. That's what the merchants pay for. I'll keep my eyes open for ones of these."

"Have you ever seen anything that looked like a forge in Khazduroth?"

The prospector laughed. "There are streets of forges. It was a dwarf city after all."

"Did they have anything in them?"

The man spread his massive hands. "If there were tools they were took long ago. Many a blacksmith would give his children's heads for dwarf-made tools."

"Could you take us there?" Karnea could not keep the excitement from her voice.

The prospector looked at her sharply. "You willing to pay?"

Karnea nodded. She was going too quickly, trusting the wrong men but it was too late to stop her now.

"How much?"

"A solar each," Karnea said. It was a lot of money. Probably far too much. The man showed a grin like a skull. His crew exchanged smiles and nudges.

"For that much, we'll carry you there on our backs."

"We might take you up on that" Kormak said. The men looked at him menacingly and did not laugh. A pretty dark-haired woman was looking in their direction. She was garbed like a prospector too. She had been paying attention ever since Karnea had revealed the rune. A flicker of what looked like recognition passed over her face when she saw it.

"When can you start?" Karnea asked.

"Soon as you're ready to go. Of course, we'll need an advance for supplies and such." Karnea nodded.

"A silver each should be sufficient for that," said Kormak, before she could dig them into further trouble. The prospector nodded all too quickly. Kormak did not trust him in the slightest. Karnea nodded to Boreas. He produced a pouch and counted out silver to each of the men.

*** 

They went out into the darkness. Kormak saw the door open behind them and the dark-haired young woman emerged. She ran down the track towards them. Kormak kept his hand on the hilt of his sword. Boreas had his dagger out. Beneath them, the lights of the town glittered.

"Wait," the young woman said. Karnea turned, her kindly smile visible in the moonlight.

"Yes, lass," she said.

"My name is Sasha, not lass," the girl said. Karnea's smile widened.

She took no offence at the girl's tone although Boreas was bristling.

"What do you want, Sasha?" Karnea asked.

"Did I just hear you offer Otto and his merry band a solar each to guide you to Khazduroth Forge District?"

"You have sharp ears, girl," said Boreas. He did not make it sound like a compliment.

"You're paying him a solar to slit your throats and take the rest of your money," Sasha said. "He'll take you up the Dwarf Road half a mile, out of sight of any witnesses and then he and his boys will show you their steel."

Kormak concurred with that assessment. He had not liked the look of the prospectors at all.

"Oh dear," said Karnea. "They are the only ones who have even come close to finding what we are looking for."

"I doubt it. Otto hasn't been underground in years. He and his boys wait on the Dwarf Road and waylay real prospectors when they come out. And that street of forges he was talking about has been in goblin territory for at least a year."

"How do you know this?" Kormak asked.

"Because I have been into Underlands and I do know my way about."

"And yet Otto has not cut your throat," Boreas said.

"That's because I know the trails to take to avoid him."

"And naturally you are going to offer to show us them too."

"It'll cost you a lot less to pay me that solar than to pay all of them. And I am not going to stab you in the back either. There's three of you and one of me."

"You could always hire some friends," said Kormak.

"My, you've got a nasty suspicious mind, haven't you? Pity it was not you doing the negotiating with Otto back there."

Karnea's hand toyed with her shawl. Any minute now she was going to take off her glasses and polish them, Kormak thought. She looked lost in thought. Perhaps she was starting to think that she might have made a mistake.

"If she did lead us into a trap, she would be the first to die," Karnea said. It did not sound like a threat, but it was all the more menacing for being spoken in her unworldly tones.

The girl swallowed audibly but her voice was firm when she said, "Yes, that's right. And if I steer you wrong I will deserve it." She paused and took a deep breath. "And I can show you where that rune comes from?"

"Can you now?" Karnea asked. Her voice was almost shrill with excitement.

"How can you do that?" Kormak asked, keeping his voice flat and bored.

"Because I am the one who found it."

"Now there's a coincidence," Kormak said.

"Believe me or not, as you will, it makes no difference to the truth. I sold it to Joaquim of Northrock and I thought at the time the bastard cheated me. Now I am certain of it."

"The merchant who sold me this was called Joaquim and he came from Northrock," said Karnea. She glanced sidelong at Kormak.

"Why did you sell him it if you thought he was cheating you?" Kormak asked.

"I needed the money," Sasha said. Her fists were clenched and there was a note of defiance in her voice. She clearly did not like exposing any weakness in her negotiating position. She took a deep breath, stared hard at Kormak. "Whatever we find down there I want part of it, prospector's rules, equal shares."

"I don't think we can do that," said Karnea. Her voice was hesitant and almost apologetic. Sasha looked as if she was about to storm away. "But I will pay you a quarter of the appraised value of whatever we find in gold. If you steer us true and we find anything."

Sasha considered this for a while and then nodded slowly.

"Perhaps we should go back and explain to Otto that his services will no longer be required," Karnea said.

"No need," said Kormak. "We just don't meet them in the morning. They are already a lunar each better off."

"Meet us at the Axe and Hammer in the morning girl, and we'll talk more," said Karnea. Sasha nodded and disappeared into the night. Kormak kept careful watch as they walked back downhill. He felt many eyes in the night.

Sasha showed up at the Axe and Hammer at first light. Kormak and the others were already in the common room eating breakfast. Karnea studied her over the top of her glasses.

In the light, he could see that Sasha was a tall, slender, good-looking woman, with pale skin and raven black hair. Her eyes were large and her nose was hooked, her lips were full and sensual. She had an intense, haunted gaze that she focused on them one at a time. She was clad all in leather, with a pick slung from a hook on her belt and a knife strapped to her thigh. A missile weapon of strange design hung over her back. Looking at it closely, he realised it was an alchemical stonethrower of dwarven make. It was a potent weapon if she knew how to use it and had the right ammunition.

"You're keen," Kormak said.

"I want the money," she said.

"You won't get it until we get back from the mountains, safely," said Kormak.

"You were willing to pay an advance to Otto and his lads."

"On consideration we might reluctantly have decided not to do so," said Karnea.

"That is disappointing news," said a booming voice from the door. Otto stood there flanked by two members of his gang. "Me and the boys expect to be paid what we were promised."

"I don't think we'll be requiring your services," said Karnea. She smiled beatifically at him, seemingly unaware of the menace in his voice. Otto slapped the palm of his meaty hand with the head of his hammer.

"A little bird been whispering lies to you, has she?" Otto asked. He strode closer, loomed over the table. More of his men entered the Axe and Hammer. The other customers, sensing trouble, buried themselves in eating their food, or scurried towards the doors of their rooms.

Kormak rose from his seat and Boreas did the same. Sasha had her pick in her hands now. Karnea removed her glasses and placed them on the table in front of her. "I can understand your disappointment but there is no need to be rude. You will not need money for supplies since you will not be going with us, but I am willing to pay you something for your trouble."

Thinking he sensed weakness, Otto said, "I think you should pay us what you owe us. A deal is a deal."

Kormak stepped between the prospector and Karnea. He smiled and said, "The lady has been kind enough to offer to pay you for your trouble. I think you should take her offer while you are still capable of doing so."

Otto was still looking at Karnea. "Or what, you will kill us all?"

"Just you and anybody who tries to help you," Kormak said. Something in his tone got Otto's full attention. The prospector looked at him as if for the first time. He slapped the hammer against his palm again. He looked Kormak up and down and said, "You really think you can do it? Get your blade out before I can smash your fool head off and kick it all the way back to Aquilea?"

Kormak said, "Why don't you try and we'll find out." Otto looked as if he was contemplating exactly that.

The barman brought a crossbow to bear from under the bar. "If you want to keep this up, do it somewhere else. Any blood gets spilled in my place, I'll be the one doing it."

"Only got one shot in that thing, Lucian," said Otto.

"One shot is all it will take to send you to hell," said Lucian. "Now get out of here and don't come back."

The stable boy and some other big lads were entering now. Otto sensed the odds were shifting out of his favour. He let his hammer drop to swing from its leather strap on his wrist. "We're not done yet," he said to Kormak and turned on his heel and left.

Kormak looked at the Innkeeper, "Thanks," he said.

"No bother," said Lucian. "Can't have his type threatening the customers. Bad for business."

Karnea coughed. "You could just have let me pay him off," she said. "It would have been much less trouble."

"No trouble," Kormak said.

"Yet," she replied. "We won't get to the city if you get us all killed."

"We won't get to it either if you give away all our money." He knew she was right but he felt he had to say something.

"I don't think a few silver will put us in the alms' house." Kormak saw Sasha's eyes narrow slightly. She was paying careful attention. She was starting to realise that Karnea was a very wealthy woman.

"Men like Otto always want more," Sasha said. "You'd only be buying off trouble till another day."

"In another day we will be out of here, if you are ready to show us to Khazduroth, young lady," said Karnea. It was odd to hear such words coming from Karnea's lips. She did not look any older than Sasha. Still, something about her mannerisms suggested a great difference in their ages.

"I'm ready to go when you are."

"What will we need for supplies?"

"It's two days to the mountain and we may be underground for a few days. Best take two weeks supply of food just to be on the safe side. Jerky, oatcakes, waybread, dried fruit. You can get them all from the merchants here. Won't cost you more than an arm and a leg."

"Boreas, will you see to it that we are supplied," Karnea said. The big man nodded. "Anything else?"

"You'll need lantern oil and lanterns. Many parts of Khazduroth are in darkness now."

Karnea nodded. Kormak was surprised to discover that not all of the city was dark. "Anything else."

"Weapons you've got and you'll need. It can be pretty hairy down there."

"I think we knew that already," Kormak said.

Sasha said, "Get your gear and meet me at the last league post at noon then and we'll be on our way."

"The last league post?"

"It's where the royal road ends and the track up into the mountain begins," Sasha said. "You're at the edge of civilisation now." She looked around and grinned. "If you can call this civilisation."

# CHAPTER FOUR

KORMAK ARRIVED AT the meeting point early, leading his pony. It was on the edge of the village. The last league post was half as tall as a man and showed the horned crown within a solar disk symbol of Taurea. It was well-weathered.

He was surprised when Sasha showed up early as well. With her were two other people. One was a pretty sad-faced girl a few years younger than the prospector. The other was a sickly-looking little boy not more than five. He watched pale faced and a little tearful. He kept glancing at the weapon on Sasha's back then at the long winding track up into the mountains. Clearly both had significance for him. He knew it meant she was going into danger.

"They're not coming with us," Kormak said.

Sasha said, "They've just come to see us off."

"They your kin?" She nodded. The girl and the little boy were watching him wide-eyed. He seemed to make them nervous. It was something he was used to. He took a copper piece from his purse and flicked it to the boy. He snatched it from the air and gave a quick bright smile.

"Say thank you, Tam," said the sad-faced girl.

"Thank you, sir," said the boy. He walked over to Sasha and tried to take her hand. She squeezed his fingers and then let his hand go. He clutched her hip and pressed his head against it. Half-angry and half-affectionate she pushed him away then bent down till her head was level with his.

"While I am gone you're going to have to look after your Auntie Sal," she said. "Make sure she does not get into any trouble."

The boy looked at her with big eyes, and nodded. He pushed himself against her then. She pushed him away and ruffled her hand through his curly dark hair.

"Don't go, Ma," he said.

"I've got to," she said. It sounded like she had explained this to him many times. She said it with a kind of weary patience. "We need food. We need money for Aunt's medicine. We need money for clothes."

Kormak looked away not sure what to say. The boy gave him an imploring look.

"Don't worry," he said. "I'll see your mother comes back."

"Promise?" the boy asked.

"I promise," Kormak said. As the words came out of his mouth he felt their weight settle on his shoulders, heavier than any pack. The boy ran and grabbed Sasha again.

Kormak stared down the main street. Karnea and Boreas walked towards them, leading mules with gear slung over their side.

"It's time to go," Sasha said. She gently detached the little boy from her and pushed him into the arms of her sister. The boy was crying. She walked away, standing stiff and straight and she did not look back. Kormak did and saw the little boy waving.

\*\*\*

Kormak looked over his shoulder down the steep rocky slope.

Varigston had dwindled to a toy town beneath them, as they followed the Dwarf Road. Tiny figures swarmed in the streets, and moved along the ridge-lines. Smoke rose from chimneys. Temple gongs tolled.

Sasha saw the direction of his gaze. "Worried about being followed?" she asked. Kormak nodded. "We left some annoyed people back there; from what you told me they seem like they might be the sort to be vengeful."

"So do you," she said. "If you don't mind me saying so."

"I don't go looking for fights. I get enough in the normal line of things."

"You a mercenary?"

"I prefer to think of myself as a soldier."

"You must be a very successful one."

"What do you mean?"

"Not many soldiers can afford a dwarf-forged blade. To tell the truth, I thought only Guardians of the Order of the Dawn carried those. Curiously enough they carry them on their backs as well, just like you do. Something about symbolising the burden of their calling. Or so I've heard."

Kormak shot her an amused glance. Clearly she knew more than she chose to let on.

"How do you know so much about dwarf-forged blades?"

"My father was a prospector and a learned man in his own way. We drifted from ruin to ruin when I was growing up. I keep my ears open. I hear stories. I've heard the name Kormak before too."

"Is that so?"

"Hero of the Orc Wars, killed more orcs than the Red Plague, saved the life of the King at the battle of Aenar. Outlander too. Supposed to look a bit like you, although the stories make him out to be a giant."

"I've heard those stories," he said.

"You don't believe them?"

"I believed them once."

"Not any more, eh?"

"Believing in heroes is for the young."

"It's a pity—this is a land that's sorely in need of heroes. The Great Comet is in the sky. The shadows lengthen. Civil war in the South. Orc hordes on the move in the east. And we're here looking for old runes in the rubble of Khazduroth." She let the implied question hang in the air.

"Speaking of dwarf weapons, where did you get the one on your back?"

"The stonethrower? It belonged to my father. He found it up in Durea. I've got few fire-eggs for it. It might prove handy if we run into any goblins."

"Let's hope we don't."

Her lips compressed and she glanced back in the direction of the town. "Yes, let's."

He let the silence hang for a moment then said, "Is Tam your kid?"

She nodded. "Duncan, his father, died last year. He was killed by goblins on the way out of Khazduroth."

"Sorry to hear that. Is your sister going to look after Tam while you're gone?"

"Why you interested?" She sounded guilty and her tone was aggressive.

"Just making conversation."

"You always this curious?"

"I am when my life might depend on someone."

"You don't trust me?"

"I don't trust anybody. No offence."

"You think I'm going to lead you down the wrong path, like Otto would."

"It would be a big mistake if you did."

"Don't worry. I won't. I want your money. And I confess I am curious about what you are doing... soldier." She placed an ironic strain on the last word.

"It does not pay to be too curious," he said. Another glance behind showed a large party on the road. He counted the numbers. They were just right for Otto's gang.

# CHAPTER FIVE

THEY MADE CAMP in the shelter of a group of large rocks, up a side track just off the Dwarf Road. Boreas built a fire from lichen and some sticks he had gathered. He did it with the ease of long practise. Clearly he was a man who was used to setting up camps. The mules were all tethered alongside Kormak's pony.

Karnea got a pot full of herbs and dried meat and some wine stirring. Smoke smudged her cheeks. The flames reflected in her glasses making it look as if she had eyes of fire. She stirred the mixture with a wooden spoon, clearly enjoying herself. Kormak walked back to the road and looked along it.

In the moonlight, he could see quite far. In front of him the cliff dropped away, falling scores of feet. He had a clear view of the road below. Beyond the path the mountains were vague bulks in the darkness. They were a long way up and the air was cold. The sweep of the wind was audible. His shadow danced in front of him reacting to the blaze of the fire. He sensed someone coming closer, recognised the tread as belonging to Sasha.

"Looking for Otto?" she asked.

"Or anybody else who might come on us in the night."

"I took us off the main road and our fire is well hid up here among the rocks."

"If he knows these hills as well as you, he'll know about this place, won't he?"

"We'll hear him coming up the road, and his men can only reach this place one at a time." Kormak thought about the narrow path they had led the mules up and saw that this was true. "And if you are as good with that blade as you seemed to think you were back in the Axe and Hammer, they won't get past you."

"Only if I am standing there when they come, and I have to sleep some time."

"Your friend looks like he can handle a weapon as well."

"That he does."

"Go back to the fire. I'll shout if evil Otto and his boys come up the path. It smells like the food will be ready soon, and you need to eat."

"So do you?"

"I'll eat later. We do the watches in rotation."

Kormak shrugged and made his way back to the fire.

"Interesting conversation?" Boreas asked. His voice was flat and there was no real curiosity in it.

"We talked about setting up watches. Sasha reckons one man can hold the path."

"She's right, if the people coming up it don't take a bow or a slingshot to him."

"If they can do it on that path in the dark, they'll be miraculously good shots."

"Or fortunate ones. I've seen some very good warriors go down to a lucky blow."

"It must have seemed anything but lucky to them," Kormak said. Boreas's teeth gleamed whitely in the darkness.

"What do you think about this place?" he asked. Now they were on the road he seemed less touchy, more a professional doing a job and confident about it.

"It is defensible and we are hidden from the road, but it would be as easy to bottle us up in here as it would be for us to hold an attacker off."

"I was thinking the same myself."

"Still it's probably better than the alternatives."

"You think our friends from back in town will come looking for us?"

"You saw them. What do you think?"

"I think they think we have money and that they want some of it."

Sasha returned and made a shushing sound. When she spoke her voice was pitched low. "If you want to see where Otto is," she said, "come take a look."

*** 

Shadows moved on the road below. Kormak could see a number of warriors and a number of mules. The men were armed and some of them held crossbows. They did not stop at the place where Sasha had taken them off the road. Either they did not know it was there or they had missed seeing it in the gloom. After a few minutes they disappeared round a bend in the road.

Sasha smiled triumphantly. "Old Otto does not know these mountains as well as he thinks."

"Let's hope so," said Kormak. "And let's hope some of his boys are not sneaking up on us even now."

"Why don't you go down the path and take a look," she said.

"I'll do just that thing," Kormak replied. He padded down the trail, silent as a great cat. He kept his hand near the hilt of blade but no shadowy figures sprang on him from the darkness. When he reached the road, the only sign that anyone had been this way were some mule droppings on the interlocked flagstones of the old dwarf path. It looked like they had indeed been missed.

He wondered how long things would stay that way.

\*\*\*

Kormak sat down by the fire, eyes narrowed and focused away from the glare to preserve his nightsight. An eerie howl echoed through the night. It was answered by another. Kormak had heard howls like that before, far to the east in the great Elfwood.

"Dire wolves," said Sasha. "Packs of them haunt these mountains."

"What's the difference between a dire wolf and a normal wolf?" Boreas asked. His voice came from further back on the path, where he stood on watch.

"What's the difference between a domesticated terrier and a hungry wolf?" Sasha replied. "Dire wolves come up to my chest and they can chop through a man's leg with one bite"

They fell silent for a moment. All of them were imagining what meeting a pack of such creatures would be like.

"They run with the goblins," Sasha added, apparently determined to lower the mood even more. "Little bastards use them as steeds."

"I would have thought they would just be snacks for the wolves," said Boreas. He was attempting to make a joke of it.

"Don't kid yourself, they are about as vicious as the wolves and they are a lot more cunning. Both like manflesh to eat."

Karnea ladled out some of the stew. "I love cooking," she said. "I am not so sure about camping."

Kormak tasted the stew. It was very, very good. "You could make a career as prince's chef," he said.

"Cooking is a hobby. I'm afraid most of my life has been spent studying the Art and the ways of the Khazduri."

Sasha spluttered food at the mention of the Art.

"You are a witch," Sasha said. There was an undercurrent of fear in her voice that was not there when she had talked to Kormak about the possibility of being killed.

"I would not exactly say that," said Karnea. "Although I do know some herb lore and I have the gift for healing and warding."

Sasha's eyes widened. If anything, the fact that Karnea so calmly admitted what she was had dismayed the prospector even more. "Aren't you worried about the Shadow?" she asked.

Karnea took off her glasses and studied them for a moment. It was as if she was looking at her reflection in them. "All with the Gift must worry about such corruption but I can assure you I am well warded against such things as it's possible to be."

Sasha fell silent. Kormak imagined she was stunned by this calm discussion of the risks of losing your soul by another woman, particularly one as harmless looking as Karnea. He was not fooled. He knew there was no such thing as a harmless magician.

Karnea did not seem to notice Sasha's appalled look. "And you can be touched by the Light as well as the Shadow," she said. "Scripture says so."

"Do you think you are? Touched by the Light, I mean," said Sasha once she had regained composure enough to speak.

"I have touched its presence once or twice," she said. "I am not sure the Light has touched me. I like to think that it might some time. It would be a blessing indeed."

"I thought the Light only touched saints," Sasha said.

"You think me egotistical?" Karnea asked. Her tone was very mild but Sasha responded in a way that she never would have to a threatening word from Kormak.

"No. I was just saying." She spoke nervously.

"Perhaps I am egotistical," said Karnea. She smiled benevolently around her. Kormak was reminded of an owl. They looked wise and splendid but they were also deadly predators. Karnea took a mouthful of her stew, made a face, and then blew on the spoon to cool it. She looked about as threatening as a rabbit, but Sasha has moved to put some distance between them. "No one really knows why the Light touches some and not others. Although some scholars claim that in every case of sainthood the one so blessed had the Gift."

"You mean they were sorcerers? You are saying that the saints were all magicians. That is blasphemy." Sasha sounded genuinely appalled. She looked at Kormak and Boreas for support.

"Some of the Old Ones have told me similar things," said Kormak maliciously.

"Really," said Karnea. "Fascinating. We have much to talk about, Sir Kormak."

"The Old Ones are notorious liars," he said to close off any further inquiries of this sort.

"Not all of them," said Karnea. "And even in the lies of the most deceitful some nuggets of truth may be uncovered. It makes the lie more convincing, or so they say, although I confess this is not really my area of expertise."

"What is?" Kormak asked. In his experience a scholar could usually be distracted by asking them about their specialist subjects. They loved to talk about them even more than they loved to ask questions.

"Initially I thought it was the Healing Arts," Karnea said, "but after a few decades I found myself drawn to the rune lore of the Khazduri. I spent some time underground in Aethelas talking with them, learning their tongue and about their ways. I am composing a monograph on the subject which I hope to have finished within the decade."

"This is why you were in Aethelas when I was a youth," Kormak said. It was odd to think that the dwarves had chosen to allow this woman to stay with them. Most members of the order spent only a few nights underground as part of their initiation and the dwarves mostly just ignored them.

"And what about you?" Sasha asked Boreas.

"I was a soldier," Boreas said. "And now I am a bodyguard."

He showed his skeletal smile. "The work is safer and the pay is better. The food, too."

"Where did you find the rune?" Karnea asked Sasha. The suddenness to the question reminded Kormak of an owl dropping on a mouse.

Sasha said, "In the Forge Quarter about a year ago. It was before the goblins and the monsters were quite so thick on the ground down there."

"Monsters?" Boreas said.

"Huge, twisted mutated things. In the first couple of years after the city was discovered there was nothing like them, then the new goblin king showed up and the tribes began to in-gather and the wolves came and the bats."

"Oh dear," said Karnea.

"You see why you were brought along, Sir Kormak," Boreas said.

"The goblins have been getting meaner and meaner ever since old

Graghur showed up. Been raiding prospector camps. Just a few on outlying tents but they never used to do that."

"Graghur?" Kormak said. His tone was sharp.

"That's what he's called. Why are you so interested?"

Kormak thought of the long lists he had memorised when he was a novice back on Mount Aethelas. "It is the name of an Old One," he said. "He hasn't been heard off since the Selenean Resurgence though."

Karnea nodded agreement. "Luzak Ath Graghur, Taker of Skulls. His worship is quite common among the goblin tribes of the mountains. Many scholars believe he was their patron in the Age of Shadow."

Sasha's glance darted from face to face, becoming more horrified by the moment.

"You are saying the goblin king is an Old One," she said.

"He may be," said Karnea. "It is not uncommon for their tribal leaders to take on the names of their former patrons. They believe it is a sign of strength."

"How do you know so much about these things?" Sasha asked.

"It's a fascinating area of study," she said. "There is a connection between the dwarves and the goblins. They are ancient enemies and have been ever since the goblins invaded Khazduroth millennia ago."

A dire wolf howled. "Sounds like it's getting closer," said Kormak.

"Best build up the fire and take watches," said Sasha.

Karnea rose from the fire and walked around the camp, placing her small rune-inscribed stones at each point of the compass. She inscribed a circle connecting them with chalk and marked some symbols on the ground, then she paused for a moment, looked at the sky and moved her lips as if she was trying to remember something. Eventually she spoke an incantation that sounded like a prayer.

Nothing visible happened but Kormak felt the amulet on his chest heat up as it responded to the eddy currents of magic.

"That should give us a bit of warning," she said.

"I would feel more secure if we set a watch," Kormak said. "No offence."

"None taken," Karnea said. She walked over to the fire, took the rune torque from her arm and placed it among the flames.

"What are you doing?" Sasha asked. She looked as if she wanted to reach into the fire and snatch the rune out.

"Mankh will absorb the heat," she said. "And can unleash it quickly if the need arises. I've been charging it for a few days now just in case." She glanced around at them and said, "Make sure you keep the fire well fed. Mankh will make it burn down more quickly as it eats the flames.

Karnea lay down by the fire, covering herself with her cloak as a blanket. She closed her eyes and immediately started to snore.

"They say sorcery takes it out of you," Kormak said.

"Toss you for the first watch," said Boreas.

"I'll take it," Kormak said. "Between the snores and the howling I won't get much sleep anyway."

No one seemed disposed to argue with him. He sat with his back to the rocks, looking away from the fire back along the track over which any intruder would have to come. Behind him the fire sputtered and did not provide as much heat as he would have expected. He supposed the rune was doing its work.

He considered his companions. They were as strange a bunch as he had ever travelled with; a girl grave-robber, a seemingly unworldly scholar, and a mercenary killer.

He wondered if any of them would make it back to civilisation or what passed for it in this part of the world.

# CHAPTER SIX

BOREAS SHOOK KORMAK awake. He rose and stretched. His limbs felt cold and stiff, his back hurt from lying on the hard rock. He got up and looked at the sky. Grey clouds filled it, softening the outlines of the distant mountains, making the bulk of the peaks difficult to see. The wind was cold and bit through his cloak. He thought he tasted snow on it and said so.

"You got the weather sense," Sasha asked as she packed her bedroll into her rucksack and lashed it onto the mule.

"No. But I grew up in Aquilea. I remember the feel of bad weather."

Karnea was mixing porridge for the breakfast. She looked around puzzled for a minute as if she had forgotten something. She straightened suddenly, tapped her nose with one finger, smiled and began to collect her ward stones, then she picked the rune torque from the fire with a stick. She slid it over her arm easily. It did not burn her. She studied the sky. "You could probably tell the same thing just by looking at the clouds," she said.

"There is that," he agreed.

They ate their porridge. Sasha seemed a bit unnerved by

consuming anything made by Karnea. Boreas noticed her look.

"She won't poison you," he said then added, "Of course, if she was going to, I would say that, wouldn't I?"

Sasha glared at him and began to spoon the gruel into her mouth. "Tasty," she said, although the oat mix was as bland as could be.

"Needs salt," said Kormak.

"A hillman would say that," said Boreas.

"Best with some chopped apple, a little cream and some honey," said Karnea.

"They would burn you at the stake for suggesting such a thing in Aquilea," said Kormak.

"It's not the only thing I could be burned at the stake for." Apparently some of Sasha's attitude from the previous evening had registered in her mind. She laughed, looked around with her beatific smile and said, "How much further to Khazduroth?"

"Another day or so, if we make good time along the road," said Sasha. "We'll be in Prospect Valley by the evening."

"What's that?" Boreas asked.

"It's the prospector's camp outside the Gates of Khazduroth."

"Sounds like a charming place."

"You can get your throat cut in there quick as dropping pennies. Keep your hands on your swords and your wits about you. The City in the Deeps is worse."

"Why do they call it that anyway, the City in the Deeps?" Boreas asked.

Karnea cleared her throat. "It was the site of the Shrine of Morakana, Princess of the Deeps, the Mother Goddess of the Khazduri. It was the largest of their cities and the one blessed with most children because of her patronage. Of course, that was before the

Plague and the Long Dying."

"They say the Shrine is down there still," said Sasha. "The dwarves still go there."

Karnea looked at her. Her eyes blazed with interest. "You have seen this?"

"I have seen dwarves," she said. "In the distance, in the Deep Dark. They avoid humans but they are still there or so people claim. You can see their sign inscribed on the walls sometimes, where it was not before, as if they were leaving cryptic messages for each other."

"No word of this has reached Aethelas," Kormak said.

"Who would tell you? The only people likely to see it are a few prospectors, the boldest ones, who go into the Deep Dark."

Sasha sounded thoughtful. "Most people don't want to think about the dwarves. We take their stuff after all. It's a kind of robbery, I suppose."

"That means it is possible we may see some," Karnea said. She sounded thrilled. "We might be able to trade with them."

"Maybe," Sasha said. She did not sound very positive. "They are very shy."

"Still dwarves are rare now in the world, and these ones may have much to tell us," Karnea said.

Boreas lifted his pack and hefted his great two-handed hammer using it like it was a staff. "We'd best be going if we want to see any of these wonders," he said.

They set off down the path to where it connected with the road. The marks of Otto's band's passing were still there from last night.

\*\*\*

As they marched, the weather got dirtier. The clouds lowered until the peaks above them were obscured by mist. The wind grew stronger and chillier, whipping Kormak's cloak around his body.

The pony clopped along beside him, hooves ringing on the cut stone of the Dwarf Road. They passed one of the ancient milestones, a stone figure, somewhat man-like but broader and squatter and a good deal shorter. Its edges had been softened by centuries of weather, and the runes along its side were filled with lichen.

Karnea squinted at them. "It says we are three leagues from the gates," she said. "It is a marker representing one of the warriors of King Malki Ring-giver. The third of that name." She looked at them all and smiled. "I am glad I came. On our way back I would like to make a sketch of that stone.

"You know a lot," Sasha said. Karnea beamed.

"I spent a lot of time in the library at Mount Aethelas. It has the greatest collection of Khazduri literature and literature about the Khazduri anywhere on the surface."

Sasha smiled as if she understood that point. "Who knows what was lost in the Underlands during the Long Dying though?"

"Precisely. I am hoping we may find some new stuff. I regret not having more time to spend in the bazaar in Varigston. Someday I'll come back and really have a rummage about."

Sasha looked suddenly wary, as if she had been tricked into talking to the sorceress as she would any normal person.

Boreas was striding ahead, gaze fixed on the road. Kormak glanced behind to make sure nothing was coming on them from behind. He felt as if in the clear mountain air he ought to be able to hear anyone doing so, but it never hurt to be careful.

He found that in an odd way he was enjoying himself. He was walking through the sort of terrain that reminded him of his childhood, and when the clouds occasionally parted they gazed down into huge valleys cleaved out of the titanic mountains. Clouds floated below them as if they were the Holy Sun himself looking down from the sky.

"What are you thinking, Sir Kormak?" Karnea asked.

"I was thinking that Aquilea must be over there somewhere," he pointed towards the Northwest.

"Twenty leagues or so, if the maps I studied before I came are correct."

Kormak laughed.

"What did I say was so funny?" Karnea asked. She was smiling, not a woman to take offence unless certain it was being given.

"The borders of Aquilea and Taurea are, shall we say, disputed," Kormak said. "The hill tribes raid across those borders at will, claim the lands are theirs and the Taureans have no right to be there."

Boreas nodded when he heard this. "My earliest posting was at Andium. Every moon or so the Wolf clans would get wild on firewater and try and burn us out. Hell, they succeeded in more than a few places. I've seen many a settler village burned."

Kormak thought about the implications of the term settler village. Even after two centuries, the Taureans called their townships on the border that. They clearly grasped just as much as the Aquileans did exactly how precarious their grip on the border was.

"I heard the Aquileans have started raiding again," said Sasha. "Have been doing that ever since this bloody civil war started."

Boreas nodded. "The mercenaries will all be heading south. It's the prospect of higher pay and more plunder. Hell, any plunder. You don't see much when you hit an Aquilean village. They are bloody barbarians." He glanced at Kormak. "No offence, Sir Kormak."

"None taken," said Kormak. "I am surprised you raided a Wolf clan village and lived to tell the tale."

"You a Wolf?" Boreas asked. "I mean originally, before you swore to follow the Holy Sun."

Kormak shook his head. "My people were Hawk clan," he said. "They and the Wolves are traditional enemies."

Boreas's eyes narrowed. "Never met a Hawk. Never heard much good about them either. Supposed to be even meaner than the Wolves."

"You won't meet any more now. I am the last." Boreas looked away, clearly wondering whether this was a subject to be broached at all.

"I've heard it said that if the Aquileans stopped fighting each other, they could probably conquer Taurea," said Sasha.

"Might be true," said Boreas. "They are fierce enough."

"It will never happen," said Kormak.

"What makes you so sure?" Karnea asked.

"Too many old hates among the clans. Too many blood feuds. Too many ritual killings. And even if some warlord arose to unite them, they would still fail. It takes more than a sword and courage to win battles."

"They help," said Boreas.

"Aye," said Kormak. "But fighting cavalry on open plains is not so easy when you don't have any yourself. And fighting a campaign is hard when your idea of strategy is to get drunk and head for the biggest town with the most loot, and your idea of tactics is line up and charge the enemy as fast as you can because you want to take more heads than your neighbour."

"It sounds like you don't have much respect for the fighting skills of your kinsmen," said Sasha.

"I have no kinsmen," said Kormak. "And I have every respect for the Aquileans. I just don't think they know how to fight a war. Raid, yes. Kill a man with a blade, yes. Fight a war against civilised armies? No."

"What happened to your kin?" Sasha asked. "Blood feud?"

Kormak shook his head. "An Old One killed them. Wiped out the entire village."

"Did your folk anger him in some way?" she asked.

"No. He is one of those who just attack human villages when the mood strikes him. They kill like maddened wolverines because they like the taste of blood."

"He left you alive though," Sasha said. "Or did you run away?"

"I was eight years old," Kormak said. "I tried to hit him with my father's hammer. My father's head lay severed where the Old One had dropped it."

Sasha looked appalled. "I am sorry," she said. "I never meant..."

"Why are you sorry?" Kormak asked. "You never did anything. It was Adath Decaureon, the Prince of Dragons."

"Why did it let you live?" Boreas asked.

"He always leaves one survivor to tell the tale. Always a child. He always tells them that one day he will come back and kill them. Sometimes he does."

"Did he tell you?" Sasha asked.

"Yes." An appalled silence hung over the small group. Were they wondering what would happen if the Prince of Dragons caught up with him while they were there?

"There was a Guardian pursuing him," Kormak said. "Malan. He took me back to Mount Aethelas. That's how I came to join the Order of the Dawn."

"And you've spend your life hunting Old Ones ever since?" Sasha asked.

"Or wizards or servants of the Shadow," said Kormak. Karnea looked away. They walked in silence a long while after that.

\*\*\*

Kormak looked over the side of bridge. Three hundred yards below the stream looked tiny. He kept walking over the great span. He was very conscious of the long drop beneath him.

"Bad place to get caught by an ambush," Boreas said. "No way on or off except to jump. Attackers could easily hit from the top of those towers."

"That's why they were there," Karnea said. "The dwarves were able to defend each entrance to the bridge and the middle as well. There were gates in each."

It was not what the dwarves could have done that worried Kormak. It was what men could do now. That far tower perched at the edge of the bridge would be the perfect place for Otto and his boys to wait for them. Even if all they did was drop rocks, they could most likely cause casualties. "Let's hope there is no one waiting for us," he said.

"If you're thinking about Otto and his lads, I would not worry," said Sasha. "They would not climb those towers if their lives depended on it."

"Why not?" Kormak asked.

"They are haunted."

"By whom?"

"No one knows but lights are seen in them, and voices speaking in strange tongues are heard, and people vanish who go into them, never to be seen again."

Karnea looked up. Her interest was piqued. "I would like to inspect one of those places. This might be the result of some old dwarf rune-magic."

"We don't have the time," Kormak said. Sasha looked relieved. "We need to push on."

When they passed under the arch in the last tower guarding the bridge's far side, Kormak sensed something. He reached up to touch the Elder Sign on his chest, but he felt no tell-tale warmth. An odd expression passed over Karnea's face, and she frowned, clearly puzzled by something. Kormak was glad when they got out of the shadow of the structure and into the cold mountain light again. There had been a definite sense of presence about the gatehouse.

Sasha smiled coolly at him. "If you think that place was bad, just wait till you see the City in the Deeps," she said. "That place is really spooky.

In the distance a dire wolf howled, as if in mournful agreement. Kormak looked up at the ridgeline from which the call had come. He saw a grey shape up there. Something small was perched on its back. After a moment, it vanished. But somewhere in the distance another howl answered its call. Kormak did not like that at all. It sounded too much like a signal being passed along a line.

# CHAPTER SEVEN

THE ROAD TWISTED round a corner and a long valley became visible beneath them, running all the way to the foot of one of the great peaks. The road ran down the slope and directly towards a massive gate, flanked on either side by two monstrously huge statues, like the dwarven road markers but on a completely different scale. Within the valley was a camp of scores of tents and dozens of other structures. Even from this distance Kormak could see hundreds of people moving around down there.

"Prospect Valley," said Sasha. "There are a lot of rough people down there. Try not to pick too many fights."

"Your friend Otto is the one we have to worry about," said Boreas.

"He's not my friend, but he'll no doubt have a few down there. They can be a pretty scummy crew."

"I am sure they are not all bad," said Karnea. Even she did not sound too optimistic about that.

"Not all of them will side with Otto," said Sasha. "He won't likely try anything too open in the daylight but things might get a bit sticky come nightfall."

"Well, we've got a few hours yet," said Karnea. "Maybe we can get underground before then."

"That might be even rougher," said Sasha. "They could follow us in and no one would interfere if they attacked us in the Underlands."

"So, it's our last night above ground for a while," said Boreas. He studied the camp in the distance. "We might as well get a move on.

There were more people in the camp than it appeared from a distance. That much became obvious as they approached. There were scores of tents, ranging from large pavilions of silk, to small prospectors tents made from canvas. There were lean-tos built from sticks, set against the sides of boulders. There were makeshift shelters made from cloaks stretched across branches. There were even a few cabins of stone and chipped rock. The camp was set near a stream for water. There were a few keen traders obviously here to try and get the pick of the artefacts early. They were easy to spot, being flanked by burly bodyguards.

As they entered the outskirts of the camp, Kormak noticed some familiar looking people had pitched tents. The squat massive figure of Otto loomed from among his hulking henchmen. They glared over at Kormak and his companions as if they resented being forced to wait here to rob them. Kormak smiled at them as they passed.

"Hey Sasha," someone shouted from a nearby tent. "Going underground again? Thought you said that, after last time, you were never coming back?"

"I've got a new crew," Sasha said.

"Tough looking bunch. Except for your lady friend. She looks tasty."

"That's enough of that," said Boreas.

"No offence, chummie," said the prospector. "I didn't realise she was with you. Still, if she's free I might be able to trade you something just as tasty for a night's company."

Boreas looked as if he was considering violence. The prospector backed away.

"He seemed like a friendly chap," said Karnea.

Sasha walked over to another campfire and squatted down beside it. "Hey, Heidi," she said. "How are tricks?"

"Could be worse," said the large, wart-faced woman. She was garbed in a suit of chainmail and had a meat cleaver within easy reach. Its sharp edge was driven into a wood stump. "Been a few goblins sighted the last few days. Those big bat things have been scudding across the face of the moon since it waxed. And you must have heard the dire wolves howling when you came up the road last night."

Sasha nodded. "Goblins bothering the camp again?"

"More and more of the little bastards show their pointy little heads every night. I wouldn't be surprised if they started doing more than sneak thieving. Bunch of folks haven't come back up from the Deeps. Jonas Tegel says there's whole tribes below now but you know what Jonas is like..."

"I do," Sasha said. "Sounds like it could get nasty around here."

"It's getting late in the year," Heidi said. "Folks will be heading back down into Varigston soon as the first snow looks likely. It'll be the little bastards' last chance to grab anything that's not nailed down. So yeah, I'd say it's a fair bet that we'll have goblin trouble soon. You here to buy?"

"I'm taking my new crew underground."

"Thought you said you wasn't gonna do that no more, dearie! I mean after Duncan died and what happened to Simeon."

"Money's tight."

"And there's a chance of a big score?" Heidi asked. "You was always looking out for that motherlode."

Sasha smiled a little sadly. "Duncan was. I was just along for the ride."

Heidi ran an eye over them. Her eyes narrowed when she looked at Kormak and then at Boreas. "Bad boys, this pair."

"You don't know the half of it."

"They're going to need to be. Otto arrived in camp last night and was asking about you, and folks that meet the description of your new crew. He seems to think you owe him money... or blood, the way he's talking."

"We're going under tomorrow, so he'll have to be quick."

"You know him. He may just follow you down, now he's got the scent of blood."

"The day I can't lose Otto in the Underlands is the day I deserve to have him get my blood."

"You just be careful of him, dearie. He's got a mean streak has Otto, and for whatever reason you and your new friends have brought it out in him."

"Mind if we pitch here?"

Heidi looked at them carefully then looked over at Otto's bunch, weighing things up. Clearly she was not too keen on getting into trouble with Otto herself. After a few minutes she said, "That might not be too healthy for me, but what the hell... you've done me a few good turns and I always had a soft spot for little Tam. Pitch away. If there's any bother, we'll see how it goes."

*** 

They made camp. Boreas set things up with an old mercenary's ease of habit. Kormak walked over to Karnea and said quietly, "Probably best if you don't set up wards. We don't want to spook these people. We need them on our side. You might want to avoid charging the flame-binding rune as well."

Karnea smiled at him. "As you say, Guardian." Kormak winced hoping no one had heard that. Karnea broke out the cooking gear and began rummaging through the supplies for food. In the distance a dire wolf howled. The sound was long drawn-out and chilling. For a moment, everyone in the camp stopped what they were doing and looked around to make sure nothing was sneaking up on them.

The howl was answered first from the north and then from the south. Judging by the way it echoed Kormak thought there might be several packs of the monstrous wolves out there. They were coming closer.

"Sounds like they are hungry," said Sasha.

"Maybe they smelled Karnea's stew," said Boreas. He looked hungry himself.

"It's no joke," Sasha said. "If those packs come out of the hills we'll know all about it."

"Then let's pray to the Holy Sun that they don't," said Boreas.

Out of the corner of his eye, Kormak saw a large group of men approaching. "Looks like we've got other problems," he said.

Otto lumbered along in the lead, followed by his crew. They all had spears and swords now. Knives were still at their belt. Otto had his hammer in his hand. He strode up to the fire, loomed over it and said, "I was wondering when you would show up. It seems like we missed you on the road last night."

Boreas picked himself up off the ground. "What do you want?"

"Just visiting," said Otto. "We wanted to make sure that you were all right. We would not want anything bad to happen to you. That stew smells good," he said, sniffing the air.

"Would you like some?" Karnea asked innocently. "I don't think there's enough for all of you boys but we've got some to spare."

Otto looked at her to see whether she was serious. Karnea smiled at him. He looked as if he was considering it but then shook his head. "You owe us money."

"Like I said, I am willing to pay you something for your trouble," said Karnea.

"You owe us more than a few pennies."

"How much do you think is reasonable?" Karnea gave no sign of being intimidated. She sounded merely curious.

Otto looked as if he was doing sums in his head. Judging by his frown, it was not the sort of mental exercise he was good at. "Ten gold solars," he said.

"You seem to have some problems with arithmetic," Kormak said.

"Maybe. But I have no problems with smashing the heads of welchers." At that moment, a chorus of howls erupted nearby. Mixed in were high-pitched tittering yells. Both were followed by screams and the sounds of violence.

Out of the gloom, Kormak could see great grey shapes of dire wolves loping.

"Wolves in camp," shouted Sasha, hefting her pick.

# CHAPTER EIGHT

DOZENS OF GIANT wolves raced in, yellow fangs glistening in the firelight, saliva dribbling from their lips. Their eyes reflected the light like demonic moons. Their jaws looked big enough to take off a man's head at a bite. Their fur was patchy. Blotches of pale skin showed in places. They bore about as much resemblance to the sleek denizens of the Elfwood as a maltreated slum-bred cur did to a Sunlander Lord's prized hunting hounds.

Mounted on the wolves' backs were goblins. Their skins were greenish and scaly. They had bodies the same size as a child's but their elongated arms and legs made them seem taller and reminded Kormak of a spider. Their eyes were much larger than a man's in proportion to their heads, and bulged out like those of a frog. There was a ferocity in their gaze that outmatched even that of the wolves they rode. Their mouths were filled with rows of sharp, vicious teeth. Their ears were huge and bat-like and turned independently, twitching in the direction of any sound. Some goblins were riding two to a wolf, one guiding the beast, the other using its missile weapons.

The invaders raced through the camp, tossing darts at prospectors, stabbing with spears. Behind the wolves, hordes more of the small creatures scuttled in the shadows, long blades and short spears clutched in their long bony fingers, capering and shrieking as they watched their cavalry do its work.

A man went down with a spear through his chest. Otto turned just as a wolf sprang at him. He wedged his weapon in the beast's jaws. The momentum of the creature overbore him and he landed on his back. The wolf's rider lifted its spear and made to stab him in the chest.

Kormak's blade cleared its scabbard and took off the goblin's head. His return strike split the spine of the dire wolf. Still howling ferociously it fell, jaws attempting to close on Otto's arm and his weapon.

Boreas clutched his hammer and glared around him. Sasha reached down and picked a brand out of the nearby fire. She began to whirl it around her head, fanning the flames to maximum incandescence. Karnea looked lost in thought, but not alarmed, simply as if she was trying to remember a difficult recipe or a complex poem. There was a look of concentration in her eyes. Her brows frowned over the frame of her glasses.

Kormak strode forward, slashing at the wolves and their riders. They parted around him seeking to escape his deadly blade. One goblin raised a dart and threw it at him. Kormak stepped aside. A high-pitched scream from behind him told him that the missile had hit another goblin.

A goblin vaulted from the saddle at him. In each hand it held a rusty blade. Its expression spoke of a desire to carve his flesh as a butcher might carve a pig. Kormak extended his sword and impaled the creature. With a screech of agony it lashed out at him with both weapons. Kormak lowered his blade and let it slide off. At the same time he turned sideways so that his foe's weapons slid past him.

He glanced around. Boreas stood beside Karnea and Sasha, hammer smeared with blood from where he had hit his opponents. Sasha whirled her brand, keeping the wolves at a distance. Otto's men stood in a tight knot weapons facing outwards, ready to confront their attackers. Otto himself lay on the ground, beneath the corpse of the wolf Kormak had killed. His eyes were wide and he looked scared that someone might notice him and do away with him. Kormak caught a glint of fear in Otto's eyes as their gazes locked. With a desperate effort the prospector threw the beast's corpse off. It was as if he was scared that Kormak might attack him while he lay on the ground.

Kormak knew he would have to watch his back. What a man like Otto feared most was usually what he would do himself given the chance. Even as that thought struck him, Otto sprang, raised his hammer and said something to his men. His eyes widened and he pointed a warning at Kormak. The Guardian risked a glance and saw there was nothing there. He turned as Otto and his lads swept towards him, weapons raised. Clearly they intended to kill him in the chaos of battle when no one would notice.

He parried the blow of the hammer, and stepped aside eluding the blow of one of the prospector's swords. He cut at the handle of the hammer, splitting it and separating two of Otto's fingers. The big man's eyes went wide and Kormak's blade slashed his throat. He lashed out killing two more of the prospectors and the rest turned to flee. Kormak made sure they were gone before giving his attention back to the conflict. He needed to locate Karnea and Sasha. They were nowhere to be seen, lost in the chaos of battle. He had been ordered to keep one alive and made a promise he would do the same for the other.

The camp was full of wolves and scuttling goblin figures. The spindly little humanoids called to each other in high-pitched gibbering voices. Kormak saw Heidi wrestling with a group of three on the ground. They were crawling all over her, trying to stab her, and bite her with their sharp teeth. He strode across and killed them with three quick strokes. The big woman rose to her feet, shaking. She was bleeding from a dozen bites and cuts. She pulled her cleaver from the skull of one of the little monsters and began to hack at a body in a frenzy of fear-fuelled hatred.

Not all of the goblins were attacking with insane ferocity. Some were scuttling through the tents, grabbing things. What they took seemed quite random. Here one danced, wearing a man's shirt. It looked like a long dress on the goblins small form. Another lay sprawled on the ground and poured rot-gut whisky into its mouth. Others were fleeing from the camp carrying anything they could. Some were struggling to pull heavy chests or large statues. They were quite prepared to face their own brethren in defence of their ill-gotten gains. Kormak saw two brawling so hard they rolled into a campfire, scattering burning wood and hot ashes.

The wolves were no different, one moment they attacked with mad ferocity, the next they were pulling forth a corpse as if to take it and devour it at their leisure. Their disorganisation seemed to be the only thing that kept them from over-running the camp.

A hail of short spears, more like darts than javelins descended in a cloud around him. He swept them from the air with his blade and looked around to see who had thrown them. Overhead he saw what looked like a flock of giant bats. Saucer like eyes looked down and he thought he heard whooping goblin cries coming from their backs. More missiles descended, hitting humans and goblins alike.

A horn sounded from nearby. Kormak glanced around looking for the source. There was a pack of goblins, larger and leaner even than the others, mounted on white wolves that looked even more fierce than the rest. At the centre was a massively muscular goblin. In each hand he held a blade. Another pair of arms were folded across his chest. A chain of skulls and teeth descended from his neck. There was a look of intelligence and calculation about him that made him different from any of the other goblins. His eyes widened slightly when he noticed the blade in the Guardian's hands, as if he had seen it before. If the creature was truly Graghur then he had. Graghur had fought at Brightmere over a thousand years ago when Areon the Bold had slain the Old One Masarion with it.

Graghur was bigger than the other goblins, almost as tall as a man, and with his enormous build he probably weighed more than Otto had. The wolf carrying him was the size of a plough horse and could not be a natural creature. Curls of flame emerged from her nostrils. When Graghur saw Kormak looking at those, he smiled, his mouth becoming wider and wider until it was larger than his head, and his teeth looked like daggers.

No definitely not a goblin, Kormak thought. An Old One. He charged towards it. The Old One's wolf wheeled and bounded to meet him at terrifying speed. Kormak prepared to step to one side and slash at its neck but, with a more-than-animal intelligence, the creature sprang to one side at the last second. His slash went wide. The wolf turned its head and spurted a jet of flame at him. It was his turn to leap as the ground seemed to catch fire around his boots.

The Old One riding the wolf let out a peel of mocking laughter. "Well done, Fenang," he said in the tongue of the Old Ones. Hearing him speak the goblins turned to look at him.

"Graghur, Graghur," they began to chant in their squeaky voices.

The dire wolf opened its mouth and let out a long terrifying howl, so loud it threatened to deafen Kormak. There was something in its eyes that suggested that it understood what its rider was saying. Was it possible it was an Old One that had shifted shape?

"Ho—mortal! I am Graghur, Taker of Skulls, Lord of Goblins, Ruler of Khazduroth and you are on my land." His voice was loud and boastful but he was eyeing Kormak's dwarf-forged blade warily. He seemed reluctant to press his attack.

"This is the first I have heard of it," said Kormak.

"It will be your last chance if you do not leave soon," said Graghur. "This is not your territory and I am bound by no Law. I am tired of these interlopers stealing my treasure and killing my people. I am tired of them plundering my domain. Tell them to go and I will spare their lives. Tell them if they stay they can expect only death."

The goblin raised the great horn that hung on his chest and blew out a long mellow note. He heeled the wolf and sprang away, his guards swiftly following, and shortly after that the rest of the goblins had scuttled away into the darkness, carrying their loot.

Big Heidi came running up a bloody cleaver in her hand.

"I don't know what you said to him," Heidi said. "But you certainly sent him packing."

"I didn't say anything and he left of his own accord," said Kormak. She slapped him on the back and did not seem inclined to believe what he had said.

"For months now, the goblins have been sneak-attacking. This is the first time they've done anything like this. It's the first time I have seen their king too," she said. "He was kind of impressive."

"He was an Old One," Kormak said. "They usually are."

"Looked like a goblin to me," Heidi said. She seemed less happy now and more worried.

"Goblins don't ride on wolves that breathe fire," said Kormak. He turned around and looked for his companions, praying to the Holy Sun that nothing had happened to them.

# CHAPTER NINE

WOUNDED MEN AND women lay sprawled by the fires while their companions tried to staunch their wounds any way they could. Others looked at toppled tents and plundered supply packs and shook their head.

"A month's work gone on one night," a man said. "Bastard goblins."

Karnea, Sasha and Boreas were standing in a cluster around their fire. They looked all right. Kormak strode over to Karnea. Her face was pale and her eyes were wide behind her glasses. Sasha stood nearby, her stonethrower clutched tightly in her hands. Kormak noticed that her knuckles were white.

"That was not a goblin," Karnea said, as Kormak strode up.

Kormak nodded. "It was an Old One."

"Did it flee because you invoked the Law?"

"No," Kormak. "Its name is Graghur and it claimed this land was his, and that everyone here is a trespasser and must go."

"This land belongs to no one. It is not covered in any of the old treaties," Karnea said.

"I suspect he claims it by right of possession," Kormak said.

"What are you talking about?" Sasha asked. "And what did you say to that goblin?"

"The goblin's name is Graghur," said Kormak, "and he is not a goblin but an Old One."

"Graghur is the goblin king," Sasha said. "They chant his name some times when the moon is full. King or not, he turned tail soon enough when he saw you."

"I think he was just surprised to encounter me, and he departed to consider his options. He'll most likely be back when he's thought things through."

"Tonight?"

"I don't think so, not unless he is particularly tricky. He gave me a warning for the prospectors. If he was serious, he'll wait and see what affect it has."

"A warning?"

"Leave this place or die."

"That sounds serious," Sasha said.

"It might be a trick," said Kormak, "or a bluff. Old Ones don't think like men. He may even forget what he said by the morning. I've known it to happen."

Sasha frowned as if she did not quite believe him. Karnea said, "It's true. Sometimes the Old Ones have perfect recollection of events that happened millennia ago but don't remember what they did this morning. Their minds do not work likes our do. Do not make the mistake of thinking so."

"That does not seem to be a very useful way of remembering things."

"They have advantages that we do not," said Kormak.

"Were any of you hurt, during the attack?" Karnea asked. Kormak shook his head. The others did likewise. "Then I think there are those here I could help."

She bent down and rummaged around in her pack, producing herbs and bandages for poultices, then she walked over to the nearest wounded man and began to bandage him. Soon his groans eased and he fell into a deep sleep. Others began bringing their wounded companions to her, carrying them when they could, begging her to come take a look when they could not.

The healer worked until dawn, staunching bleeding, cleaning wounds, comforting the dying. Kormak walked the edges of the camp, keeping his eyes peeled for any signs of the goblins' return.

*** 

In the grey morning light the camp looked, if anything, bleaker. A number of the tents had been trampled down and flapped around in the morning breeze, like grey ghosts come to haunt the living. Lean-tos had been kicked over and smashed. Bodies, human and goblin, lay everywhere. The mountains, huge and forbidding, loomed over everything.

The inhabitants of the camp had gathered around their tent. The wounded and the dying lay in improvised cover nearby. The rest of the folk stood in a circle, listening intently as Kormak relayed Graghur's message. After he had spoken, there was silence for a moment and then people all started to speak at once. Kormak raised his hand to still the babble, and quiet returned.

"We're not leaving just because you say so," said one of the prospectors. He was tall and broad, with narrow eyes and a mean slit of a mouth. He had the look of one of Otto's friends.

"I am not telling you to," said Kormak. "I am just giving you the Goblin King's message."

"Why did this Graghur give you the message?"

"Because I speak his language," said Kormak.

The prospector raised his fist. "This one speaks a language goblins understand. And he wants us to leave."

"I speak two languages they understand," Kormak said. He tapped the hilt of his sword meaningfully.

"Aye, we killed more of them, than they did us," said another man. Some of the prospectors nodded their agreement. Others looked worried.

"That won't make much difference if there are more of them than there are of you."

"What gives this Graghur the right to tell us what to do?" asked a thin, pock-faced man. Kormak did not recall seeing him doing any fighting last night.

"The fact that he has an army," said Sasha. "He has no right except that."

"We can fortify the camp," said a tough looking old man. "We've talked enough about it. This gives us reason to. If the little bastards are going to be this aggressive we need to."

"I don't know," said Heidi. "It's near the end of the season anyway. I was going to be heading back down to Varigston for the winter. I know a lot of the rest of you were talking about that. It won't do any harm to pull out a few days early."

"You mean run?" Pock-face asked.

"I saw you do enough of that last night, Jonas Tegel," said Heidi. "There's no need to come on all brave when the sun's up and the danger's passed."

Jonas looked as if he was considering a smart reply, but Heidi still had her meat cleaver in her hand. He glanced at his feet instead.

"Look," Heidi said. "We all know the runts have been getting more numerous and more aggressive these past couple years. We all know there's something going on down there in the Underlands. We've all seen the goblins and the ghosts. We all know it's getting harder and harder to make good finds close to the gates and the goblins are getting more numerous. I'm going to take what I got and be glad of it. I'm going to head back into town and sell my stuff and spend the winter thinking about whether I want to come back next spring. I'm going to head off today and I'd welcome company on the road."

She fell silent. Kormak saw heads nodding in agreement.

Jonas Tegel suddenly found his tongue. "If half of us are going there won't be enough left to hold the camp when the goblins come back. They'll have won."

"No law says you can't come back next year," said one of the merchants. "I am thinking of doing that myself although next spring I'll come back with a company of mercenaries."

That got some hisses and boos. Kormak guessed the prospectors did not like the idea of people arriving with their own private armies. That might prove as much of a menace to them as the goblins.

"What about you?" The older man asked. He was looking directly at Kormak.

The Guardian looked at his companions. "I don't know. That's something I am going to have to talk about with my friends here."

Jonas Tegel said, "Kind of strange that you show up at the same time as this Goblin King appears and starts making threats that only you understand." There were some mutters of agreement to that. This could easily turn nasty, Kormak realised.

"What did you think Graghur was saying?" Sasha asked. "You think he was inviting us all to his wedding?"

"I am just saying."

"You saying Kormak and the others are in league with the goblins? He killed a lot more of them last night than you did, and Karnea here saved a lot of lives." The crowd's mood seemed to be turning again as this was pointed out to them.

"I'm just passing through here," said Kormak. "You want to stay, stay. You want to go, go. It makes no difference to me."

"Like I said, I am going," said Heidi. "And I thank you all for the company and good times, but it's time to head back, make some sales and spend some money."

She suited actions to words and made her way back to her pitch and began stowing gear. The others did the same. Among them were the survivors of Otto's little group. They all avoided looking at Kormak now, although whether out of shame or fear he could not tell.

***

"What's the damage?" Kormak asked Boreas, once the meeting had broken up and the prospectors gone their separate ways. Their campsite was a mess and it looked like their cache of supplies had been attacked.

"Could be worse," said Boreas although his expression told a different story. "The pony and mules have been driven off and there was no sign of them. Tracks are hard to follow over this terrain. Best guess is that they're in the belly of some goblin runts right now. A couple of our supply sacks have been grabbed. I beat the little bastards away but there was so many of them they got round me. I couldn't be everywhere at once."

The words hung in the air. Kormak wondered whether Boreas was trying to justify the loss of the supplies to himself or shift the blame to Kormak for running off into the battle. Maybe it was a little of both. It was hard to tell from the man's tone.

"I've used up most of my healing herbs and a lot of the medical supplies on the wounded," said Karnea, "but I don't see how in good conscience I could have done anything else. I was not going to just let those people die."

"You used more than healing herbs," said Kormak. "I felt my Elder Sign glow."

She shrugged. "I was subtle about it and like I said, I was not about to see folks die when I could save them."

"You must be exhausted then," said Kormak. He knew that working magic drained people more than running leagues in full armour.

Karnea looked pale and there were black rings under her eyes. Her movements were slow and she staggered a little. "I can move if we need to," she said. "You said we needed to talk about something back there at the meeting and I can guess what."

"You saw Graghur. You saw the number of goblins he had with him. You still want to go below?" Kormak kept his voice level.

"You scared, Guardian?" Boreas sounded more curious than mocking.

"There's four of us. Down in the depths there's a whole tribe of goblins, packs of dire wolves, an Old One and the Holy Sun alone knows what else. What do you think?"

"That you're more sensible than I thought. I've never seen a man charge an Old One and his pack of bodyguards before."

"Let's hope you don't see it happen again."

Karnea looked thoughtful. "I expected danger," she said. "But nothing on this scale."

"You want to turn back?" Kormak asked. "We don't need to go

below."

Karnea slumped to the ground beside the remains of the fire. Her hand moved to the rune she wore beneath her sleeve. Her fingers stroked it, seemingly unconsciously. "If we turn back now, we may never get another chance to find what we're looking for," she said. "The goblins will multiply in the depths. The Old One may take any runes for himself. For all we know, that's why he's here."

Kormak shrugged.

"Graghur was afraid of you," Karnea said.

"He's afraid of my blade but he might not stay that way for long."

"I am reluctant to come all this way and then simply leave," said Karnea. Fear and something else warred on her face. She frowned.

"We can avoid the goblins," said Sasha. Kormak looked at her. The prospector woman seemed just as surprised as he was by her own words.

"What?" Karnea said.

"We can avoid the goblins. I know we can."

"There was an awful lot of them," Boreas said.

Sasha laughed. "There were maybe a hundred."

"There could be a lot more down below."

"Even if there were, it would not matter. You have no idea how big Khazduroth is. It makes Taurys look like Varigston, not the capital of a kingdom. There are dozens of levels, thousands of streets. They must run for hundreds and hundreds of leagues. A hundred goblins could hardly cover one plaza, let alone the entire city."

"They don't need to. They can just watch the entrances."

"They can't watch all the entrances," Sasha said. "There are too many of them."

"Why are you so keen to go below?" Kormak asked.

"Because a quarter share of nothing is nothing," she said. "And I need money for Sal's medicine. And I need to get my kid out of these mountains."

Karnea looked calm once more and she smiled tentatively as if her natural cheerfulness was reasserting itself. "Do you really think we can get down into the Forge Quarter without meeting any goblins?"

"If we can find an unguarded entrance, and I think we can."

Karnea said, "If we can find another of the Lost Runes, the risk would be worth it. If we could find netherium, the dwarves below Aethelas would trade many secrets." She sounded like a starving woman considering a banquet.

Kormak was not sure of this. Both women sounded desperate now although for different reasons. "I do not think this is wise," Kormak said.

"If you wish to remain here, you may, Guardian," Karnea said. "I would not blame you for doing so."

"You are not seriously thinking of going down there alone," said Boreas. He was looking at Karnea in rather a different way from a bodyguard contemplating a client.

"I was rather hoping you would go with us."

The big scarred man let out a long sigh. "Of course I will."

Kormak considered his options. Despite the dangers it seemed like the others wanted to go below. He did not like the risks but he had his orders and he had made a promise to Tam. "Very well, then. Sasha, if you can show us an unguarded entrance we will take it. If you can't, we go back."

Boreas looked relieved at being given an out. "I don't think the Guardian can say fairer than that."

"There's an old path up the side of Grim Peak. It leads to a small postern gate. I found it when I was prospecting with Duncan," Sasha said. She paused for a moment when she said the name. "From there we can take a spiral staircase down past the gates."

"Let's get going then," Kormak said. "We don't have time to waste."

# CHAPTER TEN

THEY PACKED THEIR gear and headed down the valley. Ahead of them Kormak could see the great stone gates in the mountainside, and the two massive statues flanking them.

This was the best view he had of them so far. He could see the details on their squat armoured forms. Massive runes had been inscribed on their shields and hammers, beards stretched from their chins to their boots. Helmets covered their heads and obscured their eyes. The armour did not look as if it had been made by humans. It was more angular, with flat surfaces intended to carry numerous runic inscriptions.

They were about halfway down the valley when Sasha led them off up a path by the side of some rocks. The climb very swiftly got steep and Kormak found himself scrambling on hands and knees as he went up the slope.

Eventually, they emerged on top of a large flat rock and he got a good view of the valley below. The camp looked small and distant and rather pathetic compared to the mountains surrounding it and the Khazduri statues. A line of people and animals was already leaving the valley along the old road. Only a few tents and lean-tos remained.

Lonely plumes of smoke rose above the few remaining fires. The sky overhead was grey and dark and it seemed like they were climbing all the way into the underbelly of the clouds. The landscape became even more barren. Here and there were a few small trees clutching the mountainside with gnarled roots but aside from that the only signs of life were a few birds and the lichen that clung to the stones and the sides of the grey boulders.

"I've seen more pleasant places," said Boreas.

"It reminds me of Aquilea," said Kormak.

"That's not any sort of recommendation in my book," said Boreas. He was using the handle of his hammer as a staff to push himself up.

"I suspect that where we are going will make Aquilea look paradisiacal by comparison."

Sasha was bounding ahead, agile as a goat on the tracks. Karnea mopped sweat from her brow. Her cheeks were even more rosy than usual. A few hours of sleep did not seem to have done an enormous amount to restore her energy but she looked cheerful enough. "I've been saying for a while that I needed more exercise. Be careful for what you wish for!"

"How much further?" Kormak asked Sasha.

She looked back down the slope as if trying to see if anyone was following them. "Not more than an hour if we keep up this pace. Surely you don't need a rest already, Guardian? I thought this would be a mere tussock to an Aquilean."

"I am just curious," said Kormak, refusing to rise to the bait. "Will we have time to get any distance underground once we find this entrance of yours?"

"We'd better hope so," Sasha said. "Those look like storm clouds coming in and I am not keen on spending the night getting soaked on a mountainside."

None of them said anything about the possibility that there might be goblins waiting in ambush.

\*\*\*

It was raining heavily as they reached the postern gate. It did not look like much, just a heavy stone doorway that blended into the rocks it stood among. Moss had grown on the runes in its surface. The rest of the door was overgrown so the pattern was only noticeable through being lighter than the moss around it.

There was a faint darkness around one edge of the door. "The door is broken," said Sasha. "It was when we found it."

Kormak studied the area around him. There were no signs of recent goblin passage, such as the marks of heavy packs being dragged over the rocks. That did not mean the goblins had not come this way of course.

"Let's hope they are not waiting for us on the other side," said Boreas.

"Never seen any goblins up here," Sasha said.

"Where do they usually lurk?" Kormak asked.

"Nobody really knows but it used to be you never come across any signs of them near the gate or on the upper levels. Used to be you only found them deep in the Underlands and you had to be unlucky for that to happen." She paused for a moment as if thinking about something sad, took a deep breath. "Of course they never used to raid either. Last night was something new."

Boreas used the handle of his hammer to force the gate wider and they looked down into the gloom. A flight of stairs receded in front of them.

"We're going to need light," said Kormak.

Karnea nodded and pulled something out of her rucksack. "Fortunately the goblins never got their claws on my pack," she said.

She held a glittering crystal on a stone ring. The ring was large enough to encompass a human fist, and Karnea gripped it as she would the handle of a stein. She rubbed the stone with her hand, and as she did so it glowed brighter. The light was no greater than that of the full moon.

"A moon-lantern," Kormak said. "You raided the vaults of Aethelas before you came."

Karnea made a noise of mock outrage. "Of course not. This is one I acquired for myself."

Kormak inspected the lantern. It would produce light for an hour after being rubbed or even after being breathed upon. It seemed to feed on heat, rather like the rune Mankh. It would begin to glow even if only held close to the body. Master Malan has possessed one. The light would not affect the Old Ones in any way, which was hardly surprising for the lanterns had been made by their servants, the dwarves, to illuminate their way in the very darkest places of the world.

Sasha was looking at the lantern. A gleam of avarice had appeared in her eye. "A functioning moon-lantern," she said. "Those are worth a lot of money."

"The light will be worth more to us in the darkness," said Karnea. "Let's try not to lose it."

"Are there many such objects in the vaults of Aethelas?" Sasha asked. Boreas stared at her sidelong. Kormak laughed. "Aethelas fortress is guarded by hundreds of warriors, by magic, by all manner of cunning traps. The vaults are probably the most secure place in the world."

"I was just asking," said Sasha. "I am curious about dwarf artefacts. Always have been."

"That's understandable," said Karnea with her glowing smile. "I have spent hundreds of hours inspecting the collection myself."

She looked as if she were ready to expound on all the hidden treasures collected in the vaults so Kormak cut her off. "If we're going down below, we'd better make a start."

\*\*\*

They made their way down the stairs. It was a narrow spiral, obviously made for defensive purposes. It had not been made for people as tall as men. They all had to stoop. Kormak maintained a good pace. He was in the lead, Boreas was bringing up the rear, with Karnea and Sasha between them. Karnea was holding her lantern high. They corkscrewed down a long way into the earth and emerged on what seemed a vast landing that receded off into the distance, curving away to left and right. The ceiling here was much higher, more like the inside of a cathedral than a mine.

The moon-lantern's glow formed a pool of light around them. Massive arches supported the ceiling, every twenty strides or so.

"Which way?" Kormak asked. When he spoke his voice seemed to carry a vast distance in the darkness. It sounded deeper than it normally did and louder. "Which way?" he repeated, this time speaking much more quietly, not wanting to give them away to anyone who might be listening.

"Going left will take us to the main gate," said Sasha. "If the goblins are waiting for us, they'll most likely be there."

"What happens if we go right?" he asked.

"We come to the Eighth Bridge. That will take us into the Hub. It's longer though."

"How much longer?"

"A few hours," said Sasha.

"It won't make that much difference then, particularly if it's safer," said Kormak. "Anything else we should know?"

Sasha shook her head. "Normally it's pretty safe on these levels but keep your eyes peeled. You never know. The goblins are a lot more active than they used to be."

"Last night is proof of that," said Boreas. He was standing taller now that they were out of the stairwell.

They followed the road to the right. Kormak glanced through a huge archway. He saw vast empty halls, sometimes with a scattering of debris in them, sometimes bones gleamed oddly in the lantern light.

"Duncan reckoned these were all warehouses," Sasha said, although no one has asked her. She was whispering. Something about this place seemed to demand it.

"According to Toplen and other scholars, they were," said Karnea. "Huge chambers and silos for storing food and trade goods were hollowed out from the walls on the upper levels of the city. The dwarves shipped goods out and stored food that came in."

"Duncan reckoned they grew their own food, mushrooms and such."

"They did," said Karnea, "but they needed some variety in their diet and they needed grains to brew their beers and distil their whisky."

She did not seem disturbed by the gloom or the silence. She seemed excited. It came to Kormak that she really wanted to be here, was fulfilling a lifelong dream.

"I could use some of their whisky now," said Boreas.

"Might be best to keep our wits about us," said Kormak.

They passed a junction. In the middle stood a towering statue of a muscular bull-headed man with a staff held in one hand. The other hand held a severed human head.

"Tauran," said Karnea. "The kingdom of Taurea takes its name from him."

Sasha looked at her sidelong. "A Sunlander kingdom named after an Old One. That smacks of blasphemy."

Karnea showed her dazzling smile. "Many of the tribes the Sunlanders conquered when they came over the World Ocean worshipped Tauran. He was their God-King. They called their land after him. The name stuck even after he was slain. It's often the way. You might be surprised how many of our kingdoms and provinces take their names from our ancient enemies."

Kormak paused to consider the statue for a moment. It was astonishingly life-like. It seemed as if it was just about to step down off its plinth and confront them. It had obviously been made by a sculptor of genius and it looked as if it had been modelled from life.

"Dwarf work," he said. Karnea nodded.

"I thought they hated the Old Ones," Boreas said.

"They served them first. And you can see the statue has been marked as if someone took a hammer to it. There are fingers missing on the left hand, the snout has been chipped and the tip of one horn is missing."

Kormak could see that everything she said was true. The statue was so astonishingly perfect he had simply assumed that the blemishes were intentional parts of it.

"Maybe someone tried to destroy it and others stopped him," said Karnea. Kormak could picture that; a fierce struggle between an angry rebellious former slave keen to destroy all reminders of his servitude, and maybe a builder wanting to preserve something of beauty.

"Maybe it was a prospector," said Sasha. "I've seen enough of them take a hammer to such things. Anything to turn a profit."

For the first time ever, Kormak saw Karnea look a little annoyed. "That would be pure wanton vandalism," she said.

"People have to eat," said Sasha. She spread her hands apologetically. Kormak wondered if she had been one of those who had swung a hammer.

"Why is his statue here?" Boreas asked.

"I don't know," said Sasha. "But there are similar statues scattered through the Underlands."

"Of him?"

"Of all sorts of different beings like him, half-man, half beast or monster."

"Those are most likely Old Ones," said Karnea. "I look forward to inspecting a few."

"You'll get plenty of chances," said Sasha. "There are dozens between here and our goal."

"Let's be on our way then," said Kormak.

They emerged onto an open square. In the distance there was a faint glow. The dim illumination was powerful enough to show the outlines of great buildings and pillars and a vaulted ceiling high overhead. Looking up, Kormak thought he saw a faint twinkling, almost like stars overhead except these were reddish yellow. They did suggest the pattern of constellations though. Something massive swept across them, obscuring them temporarily before vanishing. Kormak caught the distant echo of high-pitched shrieking.

"Devilbat," said Sasha. "Sometimes they are ridden by goblins. They use them as mounts."

"I saw that last night. That means they could be spying on us right now."

"Yes and be careful of the bastards. Their bites are poisonous, or at least diseased. I've seen men die very quickly, blood pouring from mouth and nostrils just from the tiniest nip of their teeth."

"Sounds like they carry bloodbane fever," said Karnea.

"Can you do anything about that?" Kormak asked.

"Maybe, if I can treat the wound quickly enough. My best advice would be don't get bit."

"We go here?" Kormak asked, nodding across the square. He did not like the thought after what Karnea had just said. Crossing the vast open space made him feel exposed. Sasha shook her head.

"We hug the wall here and turn at the next junction. That will take us to the Eighth Bridge."

"What are those lights?" Boreas asked.

"Where?" Sasha said.

"Across the square." Kormak focused on where the warrior was pointing and saw a cluster of faint lights, drifting will-o'-the-wisp like in the distance. Suddenly they vanished.

"What were they?" Boreas sounded disturbed.

"Might be other prospectors," said Sasha. She was frowning. "Might be Underdwellers. Might be ghost-lights. You see them sometimes. They come from nowhere, go nowhere and vanish as quickly as they come."

Something big fluttered directly overhead. Once again Kormak heard that unearthly shrieking. Looking up, he thought he saw a bat-like shape silhouetted against the false stars of the overarching ceiling.

"We'd best get moving." They pushed on. Every now and again Kormak looked up when he heard something large passing overhead.

He suspected they were being tracked and he did not like that idea at all.

# CHAPTER ELEVEN

THEY TURNED AT another statue, this time of a creature with a cat's head and a woman's body. She held a net in one clawed hand and a two-headed spear that resembled a pitchfork in the other. The road ahead ran through a long tunnel between giant buildings.

"Who is that?" asked Sasha.

"I don't recognise her," said Karnea. "A great deal of knowledge was lost during the wars with the Old Ones. Many of them passed on in their Shadow Wars even before the Solari came."

"Her name was Karkeri," said Kormak, as memories of a temple, a witch and an obscene rite flooded into his mind. "I met some of her children once."

The others looked at him expectantly but he said nothing. The memories the statue brought back were not pleasant. It was a tale of too many dead and yet another failure.

Ahead of them two more massive statues loomed. These were squat warriors with long beards and huge eyes, raising runic hammers in challenge. They were under-lit by a greenish glow rising from below.

"The Guardians of the Bridge," said Sasha. "Duncan always said he expected them to spring to life and challenge us."

As they got closer Kormak understood what she meant. The statues were almost twice as tall as he was but looked as life-like as all the previous works they had seen. There were very obviously dwarven warriors. There were subtle differences in style and if Kormak had to guess he would have said these were from a later period.

The bridge itself was wide enough for a couple of wagons to pass abreast and it arced out into space. The stone looked smooth as glass, as if it had melted and run and then been moulded into shape like hot iron from a cast. All across the bridge were more statues, depicting male and female dwarves in a variety of poses and garbs, but that was not what interested Kormak. When he set foot on the bridge he immediately went to one side and hauled himself up on the protective barrier.

Looking down he had a clear view into the depths of the city. Far, far below him a river of dark water bubbled and swirled. Tendrils of eerie green phosphorescence flowed through it. It did not look at all healthy.

"The books say the waters were tainted when the plague came," Karnea said.

"Poison?" Kormak asked.

"I don't know," she said. "But I would not recommend drinking from that river."

"I did not need a wizard to tell me that," Kormak said.

"The dwarves mined down there," Karnea said. "Some of the minerals they excavated were dangerous—Lumium, Netherium, Malorium. Their very light poisons a man, or twists him into something else. A motherlode of the stuff was found just before the Shadow Wars."

"I know those metals," Kormak said. "Dark sorcerers always seem to favour them."

"They have power that can be used for evil," Karnea said. "But they can also be purified. Some of them were necessary elements in the forging of blades like your own. Some of them were used in the making of runic articles like my torc." There was something in her voice that made him look at her sidelong. Did she want to find such metals? Was that the real reason she was here?

"You would know more of such things than I." She did not answer but stared down at the glowing waters far below.

"Would this place be dangerous to us then?" asked Boreas.

"If it was, the prospectors would all be dead by now," said Sasha. "Me included."

Karnea took a deep breath. She rubbed a finger against her nose and bit her lower lip with her top two teeth. "Not necessarily," she said.

"What do you mean?"

"Magical side effects can take a long time to show. They sometimes only make themselves felt over a period of years or decades. Prospectors live hard and dangerous lives. Many might die before the magic had time to kill them. Without knowing more, it is impossible to tell."

"You are saying I could be under a kind of curse without even knowing it."

"You would not be the first," said Kormak. "Shadowblights can kill in the same way."

"Elder Signs might not protect against this," said Karnea. She looked thoughtful. "I would need to perform some divination rituals to be sure and we do not have the time."

"Could it affect my child?" Sasha asked. "Tam? I was first here when I was pregnant."

Reluctantly Karnea nodded. "Such curses can take strange forms and remain in effect for many generations." Silence fell as they considered Karnea's words. Sasha looked horrified. Kormak found himself feeling sorry for her.

He pulled his wraithstone amulet from under his shirt and inspected it. It was still mostly white. The tendrils of darkness within it did not seem to have expanded. It had not absorbed any more evil magical energy since he had last looked at it weeks ago.

"Wraithstone," Karnea said. "An interesting idea. I wonder if it could protect you from the taint of those metals the way it protects you from the Shadow."

"Perhaps we shall find out," Kormak said. From where he stood, he could see there were many other bridges. Some of them were at the same level as they were. Others criss-crossed the canyon below them. Some of them were a mere fifty feet below. Others must have been thousands of feet down. The city was driven very deep into the earth and riven with chasms. In terms of the area it covered it was far larger than any human city he had ever seen.

The hellish illumination of the tainted river showed him other things. Each bridge on the far side led into a massive archway and vanished. On their side, the nearer side, looking down he could see that each level was circled by a great road and in the walls doors and windows had been cut.

A sound of flapping filled the air above. Boreas looked up. Giant shadows swept over them. Above them hovered huge bat-like creatures with goblins on their backs.

A wave of darts descended on them.

\*\*\*

Kormak threw himself to one side, arms outstretched, carrying Sasha and Karnea with him, as the missiles bounced on the stones. Boreas knocked one aside with his hammer. Two more clattered off his armour.

Sasha rolled to her feet. She raised the dwarven stonethrower and sighted along its length. The weapon twanged as she pulled the trigger. A burning rock hurtled upwards, trailing a tail of fire. It hit the bat on its underbelly and exploded, engulfing the creature in a cloud of flames. The blaze illuminated half a dozen more of the creatures. For a second the burning was so immense that Kormak caught sight of the vast dome of the ceiling far above him, thousands and thousands of tiny glittering points of light reflecting the fires below.

One of the bats peeled off from the pack, tipping over sideways and seemed to slide down a chute of air. The rider leaned out, whooping and threw another dart directly at Kormak. It flickered through the gloom, a shadow amid shadows. Kormak parried it. He caught the whiff of something nasty as it slid past his face. Poison, he thought, or perhaps excrement pushed into serving the same purpose. In any case, it was not something he wanted in a wound.

The bat came ever closer. In the bad light, concentrating on the incoming missiles, Kormak misjudged its speed. Suddenly foetid breath was in his face. Razor sharp teeth snapped by his ear. Warm drool dribbled down his neck. Claws grabbed him and, with a thunderous beating of wings, the bat strained to lift him into the air. This close, he could see that the bat had a head like a goblin's. Its whole body seemed like an unholy hybrid between goblin and flying mammal. It shrieked and chittered madly as it flew. The voice sounded like a demented goblin raving.

The bridge shrank beneath him and his companions dwindled to the size of dolls. The bat swerved to one side and they were out over the glowing river of sickly green, looking down at the hideous drop. The goblin rider gibbered something in his mount's huge earflap and Kormak felt the claws open to release him and send him tumbling to his doom. Desperately he hooked his free arm around the bat's neck, forcing his shoulder under its windpipe. He tried to scissor his legs around the bat's torso but its scrabbling lower claws kept him at bay.

His swinging weight started to tip the bat's balance. It flapped its wings frantically, trying to remain aloft and in a flight position. Its rider shrieked and gibbered suddenly terrified as they began to drop. Kormak beat the bat on its ear, forcing it to swing back towards the bridge then he lashed out at the rider with his blade but could not get any power to his thrust.

Another brilliant blaze of light and another shriek told him that Sasha had used her dwarven weapon again. He saw the goblin's terrified face above him, eyes suddenly darker than they had been, then becoming lighter as the flame-burst faded.

For a brief incongruous moment, he wondered why that should be. He considered stabbing the beast or trying to break its neck but realised that would be suicide. It was the only thing keeping him from plummeting to his doom. The bridge was below him again now, coming closer with terrifying rapidity. He swung his weight on the bat's neck, trying to guide it as much as the goblin was doing. As they reached the point of impact, he managed to turn the thing over so that its bulk was beneath him and the ground, cushioning his fall. He heard the goblin's head smash on the stone as they skidded to a halt.

He picked himself up and noticed the goblin's broken head lying in a puddle of greenish slime. The dying bat tried to pull itself back into the air, its broken wings beating against Kormak's face, sending him reeling away. Somehow he managed to regain his balance and lunge at it, driving his sword into the bat's breast, skewering it. It flopped to the ground.

He glanced around. Boreas was engaged with another huge bat. It hovered over him. Karnea hunched in his shadow, ducking and weaving to keep out of his way, while remaining under his protection. Sasha was loading another flamestone into her weapon and aiming at another bat. Its rider seemed to realise what was happening and sent his beast jinking to one side. The comet trail of the blazing shot whizzed past it and arced down to sink into the water below.

Kormak reeled forward, still winded by the impact and lashed at Boreas' assailant with his blade, shredding a wing. The wounded beast hit the ground. As its goblin rider tried to scurry away, Boreas' hammer made an awful impact on its skull, turning it to jelly. His second blow sent the small creature flying over the edge of the bridge to drop into the water below.

It was too much for the remaining flyers. They pulled up and away into the darkness leaving the humans to stare at each other in the aftermath of the battle.

# CHAPTER TWELVE

"YOU ARE EITHER the luckiest or the most blessed man I have ever seen," Boreas shouted at Kormak. He was cleaning his hammer head on the fur of one of the fallen bats. "I thought you were dead when I saw that monster carry you off."

"That makes two of us," said Kormak. He felt slow and dizzy but glad to be alive.

"Hold still," said Karnea. "I need to look at you. A fall like that could easily have broken something or given you concussion."

Her fingers were warm and they probed at his skull and then at his neck and ribs. As she did this, she muttered something to herself. He felt his Elder Sign amulet become warm against his chest. She reached out and touched it. "You'll need to take that off," she said. "It interferes with the divination."

Very reluctantly, he did so. It went against all his training to remove an Elder Sign when there was any possibility of danger, or when anyone was working magic, but she was a healer. He tugged the chain on the amulet, pulling it from below his armour, and then raised it from his neck and placed it carefully on the ground at his feet.

He noticed now that warmth was spreading from Karnea's hands as she muttered her spell. Tendrils of it slithered through his chest and spread out through his limbs. He felt a brief sensation of dizziness and nausea. It passed and he found himself looking at his own reflection in her glasses.

"Well?" he said.

"You'll live. Just minor scrapes and bruises. Put the Elder Sign back on." Karnea looked at the others. "Anybody else hurt? Were any of you bitten?"

They replied in the negative. "Good," she said but checked them anyway. She went over and looked at the goblins, turning over a corpse with her foot.

"They are ugly things, for sure," said Kormak. She checked over the corpse, lifted a badge from its tunic. It carried the same rune that had been on Graghur's horn and his armour. She turned it over in her hand, muttering something. Kormak's Elder sign told him there was a faint pulse of magic.

Kormak glanced around and saw that Sasha was studying the air above them as if she expected the bats to return. Boreas glanced behind them at the entrance to the bridge.

Looking at the corpse of the dead bat Kormak offered up a prayer of thanks to the Holy Sun. A memory of the long drop he had seen when he had first been lifted flooded into his mind. An image of himself plunging to his doom followed it. What would it be like, he wondered, what thoughts would have filled his brain in the last few seconds before the corrupted water closed over him? Swiftly he pushed the idea to one side. It did not do to dwell on such things.

"These riders serve Graghur," said Karnea, holding the badge out for him to look at. "He really is the king of the goblins."

"I never doubted it," said Kormak. "It is the nature of the Old Ones to rule those they consider their inferiors."

"If they do serve him, we'd better move on quickly," she said. "Those flyers will take word of our presence back to him, and from what we saw before, he can assemble an army."

"First things first," Kormak said. "Let's get off this bloody bridge."

*\*\**

"Why would an Old One choose to rule creatures as hideous as goblins?" Sasha asked. "Why even live among them?"

Ahead of them loomed the great arch that marked the terminus of the bridge. Rows of runes had been chiselled into every stone of the archway. Kormak could see crystal windows glittering in the rock walls ahead of them. He half expected to see goblins peering out of every one of them but they were dark and empty, save where they reflected the strange greenish light rising from below.

"The Old Ones like to be worshipped," said Kormak. "They once ruled men as false gods. There is something in their nature that makes them crave it."

"Do you really think so?" Sasha asked.

"Men crave glory and renown," said Boreas. "I have seen enough of that. Is it so far-fetched that the Old Ones might do the same?"

"I am not certain it is wise to judge the Old Ones by any human standard," Kormak said. "But, yes, I am sure this is the case. There is something in them, a lust to rule, to dominate."

"The same could be said of some men," said Sasha.

"That is truth," said Kormak. "The difference is that all men die and very quickly by the standards of the Old Ones. Unless slain, they can live forever. They can rule for a hundred generations and shape a people in their own image."

"Some scholars think it goes even further than Kormak has said,"

said Karnea. She looked almost apologetic to be correcting him but she kept talking anyway. "They believe the Old Ones created new races, by cross-breeding and by magic. Some scholars believe the Old Ones feed on worship, gain power from it somehow."

"If goblins are created in Graghur's image, I do not think I want to get any closer to him," said Sasha.

"That would seem wise," Kormak said.

They were almost through the archway now. The ancient runes gleamed above them.

Kormak tried to imagine what sort of magic could create an entire race of beings. He did not doubt it was possible. Once, in the ruins of another ancient city, he had seen how an entire nation had transformed itself into demons. If the Ghul could so change themselves, it was surely possible that their masters could work similar magic. There was something about Khazduroth that reminded him of lost Tanyth, a sense of ancient power working unseen to perform some strange and unknowable function.

"The Old Ones created entire peoples to use as their tools," said Karnea. "The dwarves were their builders."

"An Old One once told me they performed other functions," Kormak said. "That they were record keepers and lawyers and weapon-smiths."

"They doubtless did all those things. They were the most trusted of the servant races, and among the most intelligent. It is written that they were the most beloved and the most loyal."

"And yet they rebelled," said Kormak. "Like most of the subject races."

"Their masters turned to the Shadow," said Karnea. "Some of them, at least, and there was war. The Old Ones battled against each other, and their followers and their children were drawn into the conflict. Eraclius of Anacreon claimed the servants lost faith in their masters and turned against them."

As she was speaking a distant drumbeat started, loud enough to be heard even above the sounds of the city. It pulsed on, rhythmic and sinister, as they walked.

"What is that?" Karnea asked.

"I am guessing those bat riders have found some of their kinfolk," said Sasha. "I've heard that sound before. It means they will be hunting for us soon."

"It looks like they know we are here then," said Kormak. "We'd best get as far away from this bridge as we can, before they come back in strength."

They lengthened their strides. There was no more conversation as they marched deeper into the endless darkness.

*\*\**

The shadows skittered away from the everglow lantern. The beat of the drumming pounded its way into their consciousness. Sasha and Karnea exchanged scared looks. Boreas's face was a blank mask, expressionless, but the muscles of his jawline were tight and the corners of his eyes were creased. His fingers were white around the handle of his warhammer.

Kormak understood what they were feeling. He had seen ruins before, some almost as vast as this and he had marched through abandoned cities, but the absence of light and the feeling of being deep underground, amid the works of creatures who had walked this land before the coming of men, pressed down on his soul. It was an awful feeling to be so far beneath the ground and so far from the Holy Sun's light, like being buried alive in a city-sized tomb.

In the distance a dire wolf howled. The call was answered and was the start of a chorus of wolf cries that echoed through the whole city. It was as if thousands of the creatures were out there, prowling through the shadows, seeking their trail. A look from Karnea told him that the same thought had struck them both at once.

"If they go to the bridge they will pick up our scent," Karnea said.

"They don't even need to do that," said Boreas. "They just need to cut across our trail and follow it."

Kormak felt his heart start to beat faster. They could easily be trapped underground by packs of hungry wolves and hordes of angry goblins. If the raiders had sent scouts to the bridge to look for a trail, they were already cut off. He could see the others were all looking at him for guidance. If the bat riders returned they would surely be noticed. They were not going to be able to slip through the city undetected, after all. It was what he had feared might happen but there seemed no point in casting about for blame now.

"There's no going back from here," he said. "Is there another way back from the Forge Quarter?"

"The only way out I know is at the gate or the sally port above it that we came in through," Sasha said. "But there are alternate ways to it."

Her expression told him that she already knew exactly how small their chance was of keeping ahead of the wolves and ever getting back to the surface but she was putting a brave face on things.

"We need to go on anyway," Karnea said. "If we are to find what we came for."

"I admire your optimism," said Sasha.

"You sure you can get us there?" Boreas asked.

"If the goblins don't eat us first," she said. She gave a brief humourless smile as if something had just occurred to her.

"If we can get to the Bridge of Nets, we'll have a better chance," said Sasha.

"Why?" Kormak asked.

"It's narrower, only a couple of them at a time will be able to get at us. We can maybe hold them there."

"How far?"

"A long way."

"Then let's get going," he said. "Run!"

He broke into a trot and saw the others do the same. It was not easy to keep up a good pace while carrying heavy packs but fear was a wonderful motivator. They ran until the breath rasped from their lungs

Kormak's knees started to ache. He cursed the way age was creeping up on him. There had been a time when he could have made a run like this and fought a pitched battle at the end of the day but that had been twenty years ago. Even ten years before this would all have been so much easier. Now the weight of the pack tore at his shoulders like the claws of a beast. His shirt and britches were soaked with sweat. The two women did not look as if they were in any better condition. Only Boreas showed no sign of physical strain yet. Kormak envied him his youth and his fitness. He forced his legs to move and found he was moving in time to the drumbeats.

More howls rang out. They seemed closer. He gestured for them to stop.

"We can't go on like this," Kormak said. "If we don't rest we'll be in no shape to fight if they overtake us."

Boreas gave him a grim smile. Was he feeling superior because of Kormak's weariness? Karnea held up her hand. "Wait," she said. "I have something."

She pulled off her backpack with a grateful sigh and began to rummage among its contents. It seemed she was well-organised for she quickly produced a small leather package, marked with runic script. She flipped it open and a familiar scent hit Kormak's nostrils.

"Quickleaf," she said. She pulled out four large desiccated leaves. "Chew it and let the juice dribble down your throat."

She proceeded to follow her own instructions then wearily lifted her pack onto her shoulders again and started to walk. Kormak pushed the leaf into his mouth and began to chew. The bitter taste in his mouth brought back memories of other times when he had used the drug; nights when he had sought monsters in the dark places of the world, days of siege that he had thought he would never survive, rides across the wilderness on errands that required desperate speed.

At first he felt nothing. He was just as weary and it was just as hard to get himself moving again as he had expected it to be. By silent agreement, they had not started running again. It was a good thing. A mixture of marching and jogging was the best way to keep up this killing pace over the long term.

He began to take notice of his surroundings. The walls around them had been defaced, smeared with goblin excrement in places. The stonework was chipped and there were random lines scratched in the walls as if small creatures had been at work with pickaxes and blades.

"Where did the goblins come from?" Boreas asked suddenly. "How did they get into this place?"

Karnea shrugged. "No one knows. They are first mentioned in the records from the time of plagues, the Long Dying. They appeared before the city was sealed and its location lost."

"Another Old One slave race?" Kormak asked. "The Old Ones bred orcs as warriors. Maybe they did the same for the goblins."

"They don't seem nearly as tough as orcs," said Boreas.

"Maybe they breed quicker. Maybe they were intended to be tougher and something went wrong."

"It's possible," said Karnea. "Such powerful magic must be hard and the potential consequences would be unpredictable."

She fell silent as if contemplating the possibilities.

Sasha led them first one way and then another, following a twisting and winding path. It occurred to Kormak that she was simply following a safe route she had memorised, quite possibly the only one she knew through this underground maze. That was all right as long as it took them to where they wanted to go. But what if she lost her way, moved off the beaten path, took a wrong turning, part of his mind whispered.

He recognised the flash of paranoia that accompanied the use of quickleaf for what it was. It was one of the reasons he did not like using the stuff; his life was spent in a perpetual state of wariness anyway. The drug had a tendency to exacerbate his natural suspicion and raise it to the level of a sickness.

His mouth felt dry now as if the leaf was absorbing all the moisture in it, and his tongue was starting to feel thick. His heart beat faster and faster. He realised that he had not felt the weariness in his limbs for some time. He looked at the others. Their eyes were bright, and they surveyed their surroundings with quick nervous glances. Without saying a word, Kormak lengthened his stride and broke into a run. The others followed, moving effortlessly, as if they had just had a full night's sleep and were in perfect condition. Even the pain in his knees seemed to have been numbed, along with his lips and tongue and fingertips.

"Useful stuff, quickleaf," said Sasha.

"This is the finest," said Karnea. "It grows on the slopes of the Forlorn Mountain. I picked it and dried it myself."

"Save your breath for running," said Kormak.

The howling of wolves erupted behind them, closer still. Images of giant beasts racing after them, loping along with untiring stride, fangs glittering in their drool-filled mouths leapt into his mind. He could picture their light-reflecting eyes burning with the lust to rend human flesh, his flesh. He felt certain that if he looked back over his shoulder he would see them now, springing towards his back. The sensation was so intense that he turned his head but there was nothing there, yet.

He cursed the necessity of ever having to use quickleaf and loped on. The howls were getting closer.

# CHAPTER THIRTEEN

"THAT'S THE START of the Forge Quarter," said Sasha. "Once we cross the Bridge of Nets we'll be in it. That's where I found your rune."

It was easy to see how the bridge had got its name. It was a long and barely wide enough for two people abreast. It looked as if it had been partially destroyed. It was shattered. In the middle a gap dropped down into darkness. Even what remained was not solid but latticed, where magic or acid had eaten through the stone. Parts of the stonework were so eaten away as to be like a web. Through the gaps in the stonework the long drops to the glowing water below was visible.

What had caused this, Kormak wondered? Had it been some ancient struggle between sorcerers? Maybe some alchemical weapon such as acid had done this. He realised he would never know.

"Is it solid? Will it hold our weight?" Boreas asked.

Sasha nodded and said, "It will, or at least it has every time I have used it. Just be careful of the gaps. You don't want to fall through."

"There is strong runework in the bridge," said Karnea. "That's all that's holding it up. A normal stone structure would have collapsed an age ago. We don't want to place undue stress on it."

The howling was very close behind them now.

Kormak's heart beat against his chest like the wings of a trapped bird thrashing its cage. His mouth felt even drier. All sorts of fears invaded his mind: of the long drop, of the bridge giving way when they were all on it, of losing his balance and falling through the gaps in the stonework.

He took a deep breath and forced himself to be calm. Think rationally, he told himself. They needed to get across. Once they were there the wolves would have exactly the same problems crossing. Maybe they could kill enough of the beasts to drive the wolves and their riders back.

Another thought struck him. Quickleaf had its price. Soon their bodies would have to pay back all the borrowed vitality the drug had given them and with interest. At any moment, they might become too weary to fight, even to move.

"Go," Kormak told Karnea. "You too, Boreas. Sasha and I will hold them here."

"Why me?" Sasha asked. "He's the one with the bloody big hammer."

"You're the one with the ancient dwarf stonethrower."

"Only a few shots left now," she said.

"Then make them count," Kormak said. "You two get moving."

Boreas nodded and gestured to Karnea to tell her he would go first. He obviously still saw himself as her bodyguard, which was a good thing at this point. They had no idea what might be waiting for them at the other side of the bridge.

With surprising grace for a man so big, Boreas moved across the bridge, flattening himself against the sides to pass one gap, leaping over another when there was no other way to pass. He gestured for Karnea to follow him.

"I've never liked heights," the sorceress said. Sweat beaded her face and her eyes were wide. Kormak could see her pupils were dilated to the maximum extent.

"Get going. I doubt you'll like the inside of a wolf's stomach any better."

Karnea swallowed and very slowly made her way out onto the bridge. Kormak cursed again. The quickleaf was probably magnifying every fear in her mind.

"Here they come," said Sasha.

\*\*\*

Bestial eyes glittered in the darkness. Mangy diseased-looking white shapes bounded out of the shadows and raced closer. Kormak heard Sasha counting to herself above the howls of the great beasts. He picked out the leader, a massive brute whose long pink tongue lolled out over yellowish fangs. He hoped if he could kill this one and its rider it might give the others pause. At very least, he would have the satisfaction of sending the beast into the Kingdoms of Dust before him.

His heart pounded as the lust to kill rose in him, drowning out the drumbeat of fear. A savage smile twisted his lips. He was ready to deal death.

Sasha unleashed her firestone. It sped straight and true to the beast Kormak had picked and exploded in a gout of flame. The wolf's howling became a high-pitched yelping like that of a beaten dog. Its fur caught fire. The force of the explosion tossed more wolves backwards as if hit by a giant mallet. They tumbled through the air, fur ripped and burning. The leader rolled on the ground trying to extinguish the flames that were consuming it, trapping its rider under its moving body.

"What happened?" Kormak asked. Sasha looked appalled and amazed.

"I don't know. Sometimes they just do that. Maybe it was an especially powerful stone." Maybe all of the stones were once like that and had simply lost their potency over time. He had seen it happen with alchemicals. In any case it did not matter.

"That's the last of my ammunition," she said.

"Get back over the bridge," he said. "I'll hold them here."

Sasha did not need any more encouragement. Kormak did not watch her go. He kept his eyes focused on the beasts that were pursuing them. It looked like at least three were down along with their riders but there was at least half a dozen more. He counted heartbeats and watched the wolves, hoping that Sasha would have enough time to get across. He kept his sword ready to strike but nothing came towards him yet.

The riders were trying to goad their mounts forward but the wolves were nervous and snapped at the air, clearly worried by the fate of their pack mates. Kormak wondered how intelligent the creatures were. He had heard folks say they were gifted with a fell understanding that made them almost as smart as men. He had met a dire wolf in the Elfwood who was probably smarter than some of the people he had met. He fought to suppress a laugh. The quickleaf was still affecting him.

He glanced left and right to make sure nothing was coming at him from a different angle out of the shadows. Fairly soon now it was going to occur to those goblins to start tossing their darts at him. He wanted to be ready for that. He felt as if he could knock the missiles out of the air with his sword. His reflexes seemed that fast. He knew this feeling of overconfidence was a product of the drug.

"Kormak, come on," he heard Sasha shout. "I'm over."

Reluctantly he turned his back on the wolves and began to make his way over the Bridge of Nets. Behind him the wolves howled, as if they had gained courage at the sight of his flight.

*** 

The bridge creaked beneath his feet. There was an odd sensation of it giving way beneath him with each step.

Through the gaps in the stonework, he could see the tainted water a long way below. He risked a glance back over his shoulder. There was no sign of the wolves or goblins starting to advance yet, but it was only a matter of time.

In front of him was a gap in the stonework. The distance looked almost too far to jump.

Reluctantly he sheathed his sword. He could have tried throwing his weapon across but he was not about to risk a dwarf-forged blade falling into the waters below. The loss of his blade while still alive was the greatest possible dishonour that could befall a Guardian. He took a few steps back and raced forward, hoping to get enough momentum to make the leap. If he stumbled or hit the edge halfway through a stride he was doomed.

"Look out," Karnea shouted.

A wolf howled, unnaturally close. Kormak glanced back. One of the great beasts was bounding nearer. Its goblin rider had a dart poised in his hand. With a wild yipping, it let loose. Kormak watched the missile arc through the air towards him. It flashed just by his cheek, fell to the floor and rolled backwards. Out of the corner of his eye, he saw it roll into the abyss. Kormak sprang, and realised with a sick feeling that he was not going to make it. He had been distracted at exactly the wrong time. He threw himself forward, stretching out his hands, and managed to catch the edge. His fingers closed like claws. He looked down and saw the glowing waters a long way below. His shoulders creaked as he swung forward. Exerting all his strength he pulled himself up.

The mangy wolf came right to the edge of the gap. Kormak feared it was going to spring on him and its weight would send them both tumbling to their doom. At the last moment, it came to a halt. The goblin on its back began to gnaw on its ear, trying to make it go forward, chittering what sounded like curses and imprecations. Kormak kept moving as the rider forced the wolf to move again.

The wolf raced forward, legs gathering beneath it to spring.

Kormak whipped his blade from its scabbard as the wolf leapt. It landed in front of Kormak, jaws snapping, eyes blazing with a mixture of fury and fear. The goblin on its back gibbered with crazed joy as if it had taken mad delight in the wild jump.

Kormak's footing was uncertain and he was reluctant to put all his strength into a strike in case he fell. He brought the pommel of his blade down on the wolf's nose as it lunged at him.

It whimpered in pain and crouched, readying itself for another leap.

Kormak struck again, lashing out with his foot, kicking the creature. On two legs for its spring, the wolf overbalanced. Its legs scrabbled as it tried to maintain its footing. It seemed to hang there in the air for a moment then tipped over backwards. As it fell Kormak could still hear the mad, joyous gibbering of the goblin. It seemed like it was going to enjoy the long drop all the way to the foul water below.

More of the wolves crowded forward at the end of the gap in the bridge. Their riders sent a hail of darts whizzing towards him. He knocked three out of the air with his sword. One glanced off his armour. One nicked his ear, and the rest fell onto the floor of the bridge or ended up falling away through the holes. He brandished his blade threateningly as if he was considering jumping back across and engaging in melee. Some of the wolves flinched away, while their riders giggled and looked as if they were considering leaping to meet him.

He turned and ran to where Boreas and Sasha stood on the far side of the bridge. Looking back he could see the wolves racing forward encouraged by their riders.

He glanced at Sasha and then at her stonethrower. She shook her head.

"I told you it was empty," she said.

"Then I guess we are going to have to do this the hard way," said Kormak.

"Get behind me," said Boreas. "Give me room to swing. Kill anything that gets by me."

There was not time to argue. The wolves bounded across the bridge and easily made the jump. Kormak stepped away. The women did likewise. Boreas swung his hammer.

It smashed into the first wolf, shattering head and neck with a single blow. A second wolf sprang towards the grim-faced warrior. He managed to get the shaft of the weapon in the way.

The wolf's jaws snapped shut on the wood. He thrust forward, pushing the creature off balance, sending it tumbling back into the wolves behind. One was caught, the others leapt to one side and prepared to spring.

Boreas whirled his hammer, breaking limbs, and heads and ribs. Howling, the wolves scurried back and tumbled into the gap. One wolf, limping on three legs, tried to spring for Boreas. Kormak leapt forward and put his point through its throat. Another bounded over him, trying to rip out Karnea's throat. Sasha put her pick into its belly. She pulled it backwards and down, ripping flesh and spilling entrails. Kormak beheaded the creature. His blade narrowly missed Sasha's face.

"Watch what you're doing," she said.

"I always do," Kormak said and turned to see that the rest of the wolves had been driven back by Boreas fury.

A couple of them managed to jump back. They rest tumbled into the gap across which they had leapt. Kormak could hear delighted goblin squeals rise from below. They ended abruptly. He thought he heard a splash but dismissed that as his imagination. On the far side, the pack of wolves began to gather itself again, making ready for another assault.

Karnea stepped forward and raised her hands. The torc blazed brilliantly on her arm. Lines of fire emerged from her fingers and wove themselves into the shape of the rune, Mankh. It blazed so brightly it hurt his eyes to look at it. Karnea gestured and the blazing shape hurtled across the gap and landed in the midst of the wolf-pack. Tendrils of flame flickered outwards, each seeking a wolf. Their fur ignited and turned a scorched black. A dozen flame strikes killed as many wolves before the rune vanished, leaving a flickering after-image on Kormak's vision. The rest turned and fled. The smell of burning meat assaulted his nostrils along with hot metal.

"Why didn't you do that at the start?" Kormak asked.

"Didn't know if it would work," Karnea said. Her face was pale and drawn. She shook a little.

"Well, at least you should be able to keep us safe now," said Sasha.

Karnea shook her head. "The torc has discharged all its stored heat. I will need to feed it full before it can be used again." It was always that way with magic, Kormak thought. There was always a price to be paid and it never turned out quite as useful as you hoped. Still, there was no point in worrying about it.

"We've bought ourselves some time," he said, "but they'll be back."

"There are other ways around," said Sasha. Her expression was grim. "Even if we could hold them here forever they could just circle around."

"We'd best get moving then," said Kormak. "Before the effects of the quickleaf wear off and we can't even move."

# CHAPTER FOURTEEN

THE QUICKLEAF STILL burned within Kormak's veins but now his skin felt tight and his eyes as if they were full of grit. From previous experience, he knew it would not be long now before he felt the after effects of the drug kick in.

Their surroundings grew darker and grimmer with every step. Everywhere the stonework was pitted and crumbled, as if the buildings had suffered some variant of what had happened to the Bridge of Nets. Small landings rose off the street. Open doorways yawned on every side. Over each was inscribed dwarven runic script. He understood some of the words. They announced the nature of the business. He suspected that some of the other runes represented the names of the owners or builders.

He walked up the steps and looked in through one open doorway. Pipes ran along the walls, and from them came a strange gurgling noise. He reached out and touched one. It was not hot enough to burn but it was still warm. Perhaps it had been intended as a heating system. He looked around at carved stone tables and chairs. They did not look particularly comfortable but dwarves were supposed to be a hardy people. Some small knick-knacks, statuettes of what might have been deities, combs and mugs still lay on a shelf carved into the walls. It was eerie. The city might just have been deserted days ago. It was easy enough to imagine that the owners might return at any time.

He turned and bounded back down into the street.

"Looking for something?" Boreas asked.

"A place where we can hole up and rest if we have to. These places are all death-traps, though. Too easy to bottle us up in one of them. And we can't hide if the wolves are tracking our scent."

The warrior nodded his understanding.

"What are we going to do then?" Sasha asked. "Keep walking until we drop."

"Can you think of a better plan," Kormak said. "You're supposed to be our guide."

"No," she said. There was a grim set to her jaw. "Our best bet is to push on until we hit the ramps and drop down a few levels. We might be able to lose them that way."

She did not sound hopeful. Howling sounded in the distance reverberating through the Underhalls.

"I think they found another way across," she said. "Not that they needed to. We're not holding the bridge anymore."

"Have you ever seen so many goblins in Khazduroth before?" Karnea asked. "If I had known it would be like this, I would not have come here."

Sasha shook her head. "Never seen more than a dozen at any one time until recently."

Karnea frowned. "Where have they all come from? And why now?"

"Graghur is an Old One," said Kormak. "And the Great Comet is in the sky. Perhaps he has a plan. Perhaps he wishes to make

Khazduroth his citadel and is gathering his people here."

"We can talk about this while we run," said Boreas. "I am keen to put some distance between us and those wolves while we still can." Desperately they raced on. The howling came from every direction of the compass now. "Looks like they are throwing a net around us," said Sasha. "They are making sure we cannot escape. The only direction we can go is down."

"Let's hope they are not waiting for us at these ramps of yours," said Kormak.

"You're not cheering me up," Sasha said.

\*\*\*

Ahead of them a monstrous flight of stairs descended into the darkness. There were two sets of steps, one on each side of a ramp wide enough to drive two chariots abreast on. Each step was marked with dwarf runes. Every twelve steps was a short landing. In every landing was a statue, uncannily realistic. All of them depicted either an Old One or a dwarf.

Kormak took the opportunity to study the Khazduri. They were shorter than men to judge by how their statues scaled against those of the Old Ones. The dwarves' most conspicuous feature was their beards. They were long and often depicted in oddest positions, curving upwards in a serpent-like fashion as if caught by a gust of wind, or defying gravity. The hair of the females flowed in a similar way. The dwarves' eyes were bigger than humans and their ears were pointed. Their mouths too were larger, thick-lipped beneath small snub noses in the case of women, and giant mole-like snouts in the case of men. There was something about the dwarves that reminded Kormak of the Ghul of Tanyth. Perhaps they came from the same stock, modified in a different way by the sorcery of the Old Ones.

The women were mostly robed, the males were mostly armoured, save for a few who held scrolls and appeared to be on the verge of making speeches.

The stairs ran down a long way, and the path was perfectly straight. They had barely reached the bottom when a chorus of howls broke out from the top. Glancing back Kormak saw a pack of wolves and riders massing at the top of the stairs. There were scores of them, too many to fight, and they were getting ready to charge.

Kormak considered making a stand but it seemed hopeless. Sasha had already broken into a run and was heading out of sight. Boreas and Karnea were following her. The goblin leader was addressing his troops. Kormak left him to it and raced after the rest.

Bones were scattered around the place. They crunched under his boots or skittered away at the passage of his flying feet. Most were goblin-sized but there were skeletons of wolves and larger creatures that were definitely not goblins. The bones were crushed and splintered. There were fewer skulls than he would have expected.

The howling behind him drove him on. He risked a glance over his shoulder. The wolves and their riders had stopped at the foot of the stairs. The wolves bayed with hunger and wrath, the goblins brandished their weapons and chittered threats. None of them made any move further.

Up ahead, Sasha and the others had halted. A few goblins lobbed futile missiles in their direction but none of them made any attempt to come any further.

"They've stopped," said Karnea. A frown furrowed her brow.

"They almost had us," said Sasha. "Why did they quit now?"

"Maybe they are afraid of something," said Boreas.

"What could there possibly be around here that would frighten off a warband like that?" Sasha said.

"Let's hope we don't find out," said Kormak. He sniffed the air. There was a foetid scent to it.

"The way our luck has been going I am not too hopeful of that."

A goblin larger than the others strode along the front of their line, berating them, but it was clear that the other goblins were refusing to follow.

Somewhere in the depths, an unholy bellow sounded, as if some great beast had sensed the presence of intruders and was warning them from its territory.

"I hate it when I am right," said Boreas.

*-*-*

They trudged deeper into the district, determined to put the goblins behind them. The others all seemed to feel that they would be safer with the wolves and their riders out of sight.

Their feet scuffed along the ground as if they were too heavy to lift. The unnatural energy of the quickleaf drained from Kormak's body. His limbs felt stiff and achy, as if he were coming down with a disease. Dire fears of the creature that had made that awful sound scuttled through his mind but they had heard nothing more since the initial bellow.

"We need to find a place to rest," he said. Boreas nodded agreement. Sasha grunted. Karnea reeled along as if lost in a world of fatigue. He raised his hand as a sign that they should stop. If they blundered into whatever had frightened off the goblins, they were most likely dead.

They were trudging along a street of open-fronted shops. There were no goods, only trash strewn about. They were of a shophouse design with living quarters at the back. Kormak shepherded the party into the storefront and through into the sleeping area. He chose at random but that was as good as anything else at the moment.

The others threw their packs on the ground and collapsed on top of them, using them as pillows. The drums still sounded. The vibration could be felt through the floor.

Karnea lay on her back, staring at the ceiling. "This is not quite turning out the way I thought it would," she said. She sounded as if she wanted to cry.

"We're not dead yet," said Boreas. He clearly meant it to sound encouraging but it just reminded everyone of how close they had come to meeting their fates.

"We're all suffering from the after-effects of quickleaf," Kormak said. "Get some rest. Things will look better after some sleep."

"We need to set watches," said Boreas.

"I will take the first," said Kormak. The warrior nodded agreement and slumped down gratefully. All of the others closed their eyes. Soon Boreas was snoring. Kormak sat facing the door, with his back to the wall, scabbarded blade across his knees. He found his thoughts drifting.

It had been a very long day. The events on the surface seemed a long time ago, as if they had happened weeks ago and not... He had no idea how many hours it had been since they started. If forced to guess, he would say that the sun had set above.

"What are you thinking?" Sasha asked softly.

"I thought you were going to get some sleep."

"I can't get my mind to stop." She looked enviously at the snoring Boreas and Karnea who lay with her head atop her arm, propped up against her pack, the very picture of exhaustion.

"It happens," said Kormak.

"Are you always like this? I've seen stones show more emotion."

"Well, we are in a dwarven city."

"Was that supposed to be a joke?"

"They are good sculptors," he said. "They can make stonework show emotion."

"I knew what you were trying to say. There's no need to bludgeon me over the head with it."

He shrugged.

"I am sorry," she said. "I am just nervous. Hell, more than that... I am terrified."

"That's understandable."

"You don't think we're going to get out of here alive, do you?"

"I've survived worse places than this."

She studied him for a moment, head tilted to one side. "You have, haven't you? You're not just saying that."

"I thought I was going to die today," he said. "Several times. I am still here. The same may be true tomorrow."

"Or it may not."

He smiled. "Or it may not. I have lived with the prospect of death since I was eight years old. I don't find it as frightening as I once did."

"Since... since the Old One came to your village?"

"Yes."

She moved a little closer, placed her head against his shoulder. She was seeking comfort. He measured the distance to the door, decided he could push her off and get to his feet before anyone could reach him. The pressure of her head comforted him too.

"It's not me so much I am worried about—all right, that's a lie, I am worried about me—but I am really scared for Tam and Sal. What will happen to them if I don't come back?"

"They'll survive. I did."

"You had Master Malan to look after you." Kormak thought about that. He remembered how invincible Malan had seemed, so stern and just but reassuring at the same time.

"True."

"If anything happened to me down here, there will be no one to look after them. Tam needs medicine. Sal can barely look after herself."

He looked down at her. There were tears running down her face. She was fighting back sobs.

"Nothing's going to happen to you. I won't let it. I gave Tam my promise."

"You could at least try and sound convincing," she said.

"I am not likely to come back if you don't."

"That's much more convincing and even less reassuring."

"Apparently, I am not very good at this."

"You are a little too honest."

"You think?" Kormak thought of the many deceptions his life as a Guardian had forced him to perform, the many lies he had told to people he had later killed. Her words seemed like a joke to him and he was about to say so then he noticed her breathing was soft. Her eyes were closed. She was asleep. Exhaustion had finally caught up with her.

Kormak gently laid her head down on his pack, shifted his weight and kept his eyes on the door. He thought about young Tam. He thought about his own father. He thought about oaths he had sworn and promises he had made. Sasha had not taken his words seriously but he had meant them. If he could he would keep her alive. Now the only question was who was going to do the same for him?

Tired as he was, he stood guard until his watch was over. Only when Boreas had woken himself did he allow himself to drop headlong into deep, deep sleep.

# CHAPTER FIFTEEN

KORMAK SAW THE city as it had once been. The streets teemed with dwarves, proud and noble. They were broad and powerful and they did not walk like men. Sometimes they lowered their long, strong arms to the ground and moved on all fours. Around the dwarves, moving in packs, were numerous other creatures, smaller, with tiny bodies and spindly limbs, adapted to moving through the narrow pipes and corridors, working at tens of thousands of menial tasks. There was something familiar about them suggestive of goblins, although these small beings were less savage, more docile, seemingly happy with their work and the positions of utter servitude. Among them, the Old Ones stalked like princes, surrounded by retinues of creatures glittering and monstrous, none more so than themselves.

Kormak knew he was dreaming. He wondered if he was seeing something real, some echo of the past caught within the endless geomantically shaped corridors of the city, or whether this had all been conjured up out of his own mind from the sights he had witnessed. The thought vanished, forgotten instantly as the scene changed.

War came to the world outside the city. The Old Ones fought among themselves with terrible weapons. Refugees sought sanctuary in Khazduroth bearing the seeds of its destruction. Plague was unleashed and the dwarves died. Their small servants changed. They had become smaller of head and torso, longer and spindlier of limb. They seemed more and more numerous as if breeding faster and faster.

There were fewer and fewer Old Ones present and those who remained looked different, more brutal, as if they had adapted themselves to war. There were fewer dwarves too and they looked haggard and haunted as the war raged on through their city. They wore armour now and they carried weapons that blazed with terrible runes. Madness took them and they fought with each other. Some fled the city through the open gates. Some stayed and were changed utterly.

Years became decades. Decades became centuries. Hordes of monstrously mutated menials and companies of armoured dwarves stalked through the near-abandoned city. The lights were dim. Many of the potent runestones had been defaced. Rubble blocked streets as if the whole place had been hit by an earthquake. He knew somehow that the destruction had affected the potent geomancies of the city, blocked the flows of magical energy, tainted them, added to the deaths and mutations.

The war built to a blazing crescendo. The dwarves were led now by a single surviving Old One. The menials by another. Both of them were changed from what they had been. The female leading the dwarves looked pale and ill although she still blazed with magical power. The male leading the mutated menials looked ever more like them but far larger, and he bore more than a passing resemblance to Graghur. The two Old Ones fought with the intensity of lovers turned enemies. The one that might have been Graghur wounded the female with a terrible runic weapon. She in turn cursed him with a power and vehemence that sent him fleeing from the city, filled with terror, body becoming ever more twisted.

The scene shifted again and Kormak felt as if he was on the verge of witnessing some new momentous change, but then the whole city began to shake once more as if in the grip of an earthquake. In the distance he could hear the sound of a great heartbeat, shaking the entire world so violently that it threatened to tumble apart. The vibration was so great that it swept him from side to side as he fell, battering him off the walls as he tumbled.

Mighty winds roared in his ears. They buffeted him relentlessly. The wind howled louder than any wolf and he realised at last that it was howling his name.

"Kormak," it said as he slammed against a wall and burning lava rose to greet him.

"Kormak," it said as a stone floor gave way beneath him, sending a sulphurous cloud up to greet him.

"Kormak," it said. He looked up into the face of Karnea as he came awake.

"What is it?" Kormak swallowed. His mouth felt dry. His limbs felt weak. His neck felt tense. He rose, realising that he still clutched the blade in his hand.

"You were talking in your sleep," she said. "In the Old Tongue."

"What was I saying?"

"You talked about Graghur and menials and war."

"I was dreaming," he said, and told her what he had seen.

She tilted her head and looked at him oddly. "Have you had such dreams before?

"Yes. In the past. In other places. Why?"

"Where you have dreamed of things that happened in the deep past?"

"This was just a nightmare. Brought on by this place."

"Maybe," she said. "Or maybe you are a sensitive. One of those who soaks up the events in a place."

"I am no sorcerer, no diviner either."

"It's a gift some have," Karnea said. "It's not like casting a spell. Sometimes it only works when the conscious mind is at rest. Tell me honestly, do you think what you witnessed in your dream happened?"

He considered denying it. "It might have."

She smiled at his surly tone. "Maybe you're right. Maybe it was just a dream."

A sound came through the open doorway, a sort of heavy slithering.

"Perhaps you should have paid more attention to our surroundings and less to what I was saying," Kormak said. "You were on watch."

Karnea looked guilty and moved over to Boreas to wake him.

Kormak rose and stalked to the entrance and looked out. Something massive moved by in the gloom. A long snake-like torso was visible on the street outside. A mouldy stink filled the air. He slid forward into the open shopfront, sword held ready.

He looked out and saw an immense serpent. Where the head would have been on a snake there was what, at first, looked like a human torso. It might have belonged to a muscular giant of a man, except that the head was the wrong shape. It had the huge bat-like ears of a goblin and the shimmering scaly skin. It was an unholy combination of goblin and devil python and something else, a Shadow demon perhaps.

Behind it was a trail of foul-smelling slime. Its head turned and it looked back and Kormak ducked out of its line of sight. He had a brief glimpse of whitish blind-seeming eyes.

The snake thing halted. Kormak wondered whether he had been seen. His one consolation was that if he had been, the monster would have great difficulty finding its way into this cramped space. Not that it needed to, he realised. It could simply wait for them to emerge or die of starvation. Clearly this was something the goblins feared and it must be even more formidable than it looked to have frightened them.

Kormak pressed his back against the wall of the shop front and held very still. He could hear only distant beating of goblin drums. Was the creature waiting to see what he was doing or was it, even now, gliding silently closer?

He fought down the near-suicidal urge to stick his head out and take a look. Long minutes dragged by. Boreas emerged from the inner chamber and looked at Kormak enquiringly. Kormak gestured a warning for him to stay where he was and not make any noise.

He waited a while longer and remained still. The slithering started once more and slowly receded into the distance. Boreas emerged from the inner chamber. Sasha followed him.

"What was that thing?" Boreas asked.

"I don't know," Kormak said. "I've not see its like before."

"How did it not notice us," Sasha said. She gestured back to the doorway. The light of the everglow lantern was faint but in the dark it might as well have been a beacon.

"Sometimes the Old Ones and their creatures do not see as we do. Perhaps it was blind to ordinary light."

"It's very possible," said Karnea emerging from the chamber. "After all, what use do creatures who dwell in darkness have for eyes?"

"The goblins have eyes," said Sasha. "The dwarves, too, if those statues are correct."

"I was merely offering a suggestion," Karnea said. She glanced over at Kormak, clearly made nervous by what she was about to say. Since they had ventured underground she had lost her natural cheerfulness. "This is where we are supposed to look for what we came for, Sir Kormak. I confess it all seemed much easier when we were outside. I had no idea how vast this place is. No, let me rephrase that. In my mind, I knew how big it was, but there is a difference between knowing something intellectually and experiencing it."

"You mean we were going to have to search this whole place?" Sasha said. "Looking for clues to these runes you seek?"

Karnea nodded.

"Don't you have some magic that will help you? An amulet of divination, a spell, a familiar that can sniff the stuff out?"

Karnea took off her glasses and began to polish them furiously. "I know what we are looking for can mostly likely be found in the smithies of the Forge Quarter." She took a blade and scratched a rune on the floor, a stylised hammer inside a triangle. "This is the symbol we are looking for. The places will have anvils and forges in the dwarven style. Your father was a blacksmith, I believe, Sir Kormak so I can assume you know what we are looking for."

Kormak looked at her sidelong. She seemed entirely serious. Maybe she was nervous and gabbling. Maybe Sasha's attitude had annoyed her. Or maybe it was some sort of hangover from the quickleaf.

"What about the monster? It seems to roam the area. If so many goblins are afraid of it, we should be too."

"It does not appear to be too bright," said Karnea. "We should be able to hear it as it approaches and if we keep a watch we should be able to flee from it."

"That seems like a long shot," said Sasha.

"What would you have us do? We must at least make an attempt to find what we came for." She looked at Kormak to confirm this. He guessed she was not quite as certain of that as she sounded. He nodded.

"Of course, there may be more than one of the beasts," he said. "We can't just make the assumption that it's solitary."

"Always look on the bright side, eh Sir Kormak," said Boreas.

"Better to prepare for the worst," said Kormak. "I have a feeling this is the sort of place that is going to throw it at us."

"I don't think you are wrong," said Boreas.

"What about water?" Kormak asked. "If we're stuck down here for long we will need it more than food, or at least long before we need food."

Sasha said, "There are fountains in the plazas and squares. Some of them still work. There will be edible fungi."

"We'll need to find water that is not tainted," Kormak said.

"I can perform a suitable divination if it comes to that," said Karnea.

"Well, let's keep our eyes peeled for a fountain as well as shops marked with the hammer rune."

As they shouldered their packs and prepared to leave, Kormak wondered about his dream. He had experienced such things before and they had sometimes been proven true. Was that the case now or the whole thing was just a product of his feverish imagination and the after-effects of the quickleaf? Or was Karnea right about him having some sort of sensitivity to his surroundings. He pushed the thought aside. He had other things to worry about right now.

They emerged cautiously onto the street. Kormak inspected the slime trail left behind by the serpent creature. It was already starting to dry out, leaving a sticky glaze on the hard rock of the floor.

Karnea knelt over it and smelled it. She wrinkled her nose. "Pungent," she said. "But odd, snakes are normally dry skinned. Why would it leave such a trail?" She seemed to be asking the question more of herself than anyone else. No one tried to answer.

"At least we'll know where the thing has been. Maybe we can figure out the extent of its territory," said Boreas.

"Let's just try and keep out of its way," said Kormak. They moved off along the corridor, moving in a small pool of dim light. They could tell the edge of the Forge Quarter by the glimmer of green light at its edges but that did not help them much up close.

It was a long, slow tedious process moving along each street, checking the runes above every arch and then when they found shops bearing the sign they were looking for, entering and searching them. It was not helped by the fact that they had to change routes when they heard the bellow of the serpent creature and of something else, equally as menacing. Sometimes they went down ramps and the buildings took on multiple levels above them. Kormak was sure there was a pattern to it but it was not one he could see. In the distance something huge roared.

There were other shrieks and thunderous rumbles, all in a different tone from that of the creature they had seen. There was definitely more than one monster loose in the Forge Quarter and more than one type. Kormak wondered if they were all as large and deadly as the first one he had seen.

"You ever heard of these creatures before?"

"Monsters? In the Forge Quarter?" Sasha replied. "No, though I'd heard they dwelled deep down, far below us and hardly ever came to the upper levels."

"Maybe something is driving them up," said Boreas, a little too cheerfully for Kormak's liking.

"I don't want to think of anything that could frighten that serpent beast," said Sasha.

Boreas grinned. "It's best to prepare for the worst. As a wise man once said." She grinned back at him although on her the expression looked sickly.

"Let's get on with it," Kormak said.

# CHAPTER SIXTEEN

AHEAD OF THEM the sounds of combat rang out. There were bellows of rage interspersed with the impact of something heavy on flesh. There was something else too, the sound of someone almost human shouting out in a tongue that was strangely familiar.

Karnea's hand fell on his shoulder, "That is a dwarvish battle-cry," she said.

Of course. He had heard such a voice before in the mines below Mount Aethelas. It was deeper than any human's, with a much richer timbre.

"He sounds like he's having a hard time," said Kormak. "If one of those monsters has caught him, there's not much we can do."

Karnea shot him a reproachful look. "Think, Sir Kormak. A living dwarf. A native of Khazduroth. Who knows what he might be able to tell us?"

"We won't be able to listen if we are dead," said Kormak.

"You are a Guardian of the Dawn," said Karnea. "You were trained to fight monsters."

"I prefer fights I can win," said Kormak. "And we are here to find these runes of yours."

"This dwarf might be able to help us do that," said Sasha.

Kormak moved in the direction of the combat. "Stay behind me," he told Boreas.

He rounded the corner and was confronted by a battle, but not the one he had been expecting. The serpent thing was fighting with a creature equally as huge. This one was more than twice the height of a man, a bat-eared, scaly skinned abomination that might have been a cross between a goblin and a giant. It clutched a monstrous axe in one mighty hand. On its head was a horned helmet. Its eyes glowed a sickly yellow. Two huge tusks protruded from its lower lip. It was keeping the serpent thing at bay with sweeps of its club. Its opponent slithered forward, its sinuous body writhing on the slippery slime trail it created.

Kormak looked for the dwarf who had been shouting, fearing that he was already dead. Eventually he saw the small figure, backed into a doorway, sheltering from the conflict. Kormak had the vague impression of a figure almost as broad as it was tall, bearded, half-naked, armed with a hammer and a shield, skin marked with tattoos, a massive horn slung from his neck.

The yellow-eyed giant lunged forward, cleaving the serpent thing's flesh. It got a massive coil in the way and let out a bellow of pain as the axe impacted, drawing blood. The giant howled triumphantly and raised its axe for another blow. The snake creature moved with lightning speed, looping around the giant's body. The giant still had his arm free and brought his weapon down, but the angle was wrong, and his blow fell on the back and shoulder of the serpent thing. Bone cracked but the serpent did not let go of its tenacious grip. It looped more and more of its coiled length around the giant and began to squeeze.

Sensing its peril too late, the entrapped victim let go of its weapon and tried to wrestle its way free. Its hands were big enough to grasp a man around the chest, and its muscles looked powerful enough to uproot trees but it could not get a good grip on the slime-coated coils draping its body. It reached out for the serpent thing's throat. Its opponent weaved its upper body from side to side, avoiding having those shovel-like hands wrapped round its neck, all the time squeezing and squeezing with tremendous force.

The giant's glowing eyes bulged. The tendons on its neck stood out like ships rigging drawn taut in a storm. Something cracked, perhaps a rib. The giant let out a high-pitched scream of agony. The serpent creature looped more and more coils around its weakening foe. The grinding, cracking sound continued and the giant began to flop helplessly, bones broken, spine shattered. Pungent death stink filled the air. Excrement and piss spattered the ground beneath it.

Kormak raced forward and leapt, slashing at the serpent thing's neck, aiming for the spinal column. His dwarf-forged blade sliced flesh and cut through bone. The monster spasmed, coils unwinding themselves from around the body of its dead foe. Kormak rolled clear as the huge whip of muscle lashed randomly about. The serpent thing was probably as deadly in its death agonies as it ever had been in life, and Kormak was careful to keep himself out of its reach.

After a few minutes the violent flailing died away. The serpent thing lay still. The dwarf emerged from the archway in which it had been sheltering.

***

Karnea managed to get to the dwarf before Kormak did. She bounded passed the still-twitching corpse of the serpent thing and picked her way around the jellied remains of the giant to do so. She stood confronting the dwarf who stared back at her.

Kormak got to her side as fast as he could and studied the dwarf. He came only about halfway up Kormak's chest but he was much broader. His arms were longer than a man's and as muscular as a blacksmiths. His legs were short in proportion to his size. He was wearing leather britches and boots but his whole massively muscular upper body was naked, revealing detailed tattoos of dwarf runes. His beard was what held Kormak's attention though. It was long and loose and ran almost to his belt. It swayed even though there was not a hint of a breeze. It reminded Kormak uncomfortably of the movement of the serpent thing.

"You killed the Slitherer," said the dwarf. His language sounded very much like the tongue of the Old Ones. His voice was as deep and rich. There was a strange undertone to it though. In a man, Kormak would have said, of hysteria, but he did not know dwarves well enough to judge whether this was the case. "You bear one of the forbidden weapons."

His great blind-seeming eyes focused on Kormak's sword. His beard rippled, each individual hair like a tiny snake. Now that he was close enough Kormak could see that it was not composed of hairs but of almost translucent tubes.

The dwarf's face superficially resembled that of a human. The eyes were much larger than a man's. There seemed to be no whites and the only indication of a pupil and retina was an area darker than the rest. The ears were large and pointed. The nose was massive and broad, flattened against the face with huge nostrils. The mouth was wide. The teeth were like tombstones. A large rune had been tattooed in the middle of the dwarf's forehead. More had been inscribed beneath his eyes.

"Greetings, Child of Stone," said Karnea. The dwarf's mouth fell open. His hand went to the great horn hanging from his neck as if he was considering sounding it and summoning help.

"You speak the Mother's Tongue," he said. His accent was strange to Kormak's ears and the words sounded slurred and mangled. He had some difficulty understanding what the dwarf was saying.

"Not well but I have been taught it," Karnea said. "Taught it by dwarves."

She spoke very slowly and very clearly and it came to Kormak that she was having the same difficulty he was, and expected the dwarf to be having the same.

"Why would any of the People teach a Shadow worshipper?" The dwarf's words were blunt. There did not seem to be any malice in them. It was as if he was unaware that he was making an accusation that could get him killed.

"We are not followers of the Shadow," Karnea said. The dwarf tilted his head to one side. His grip on his axe tightened.

"All who dwell outside the Hold are worshippers of the Shadow," he said.

"That is not true," said Karnea.

"What are they saying?" Sasha asked Kormak. Kormak told her, dividing his attention between speaking to her and listening to what Karnea and the dwarf were talking about.

"He bears one of the forbidden blades," said the dwarf. A nod of his head indicated Kormak. "One that bears the runes for Chaos and Death. They spell out a sentence of death for the Eldrim." Eldrim was what the Old Ones called themselves. Their servants did too.

"It is a weapon consecrated to the service of Holy Sun," said Kormak.

"The Sun was never our friend," said the dwarf. "Nor the friend of those we once served."

"Nor was he ever allied with the Shadow," said Kormak.

"There may be truth in what you say," said the dwarf.

"Why do you call the sword a forbidden weapon?" Karnea asked. "It was forged by your kin."

"Not by my kin," said the dwarf. "I belong to the Faithful. We have kept our oaths."

Kormak was starting to realise that he did not understand dwarvish history as well as he thought. Clearly this powerful, primitive-looking creature had a different understanding of the world than the dwarves who were allied to his order. He bore no resemblance to the proud warriors the statues depicted either. He looked like a barbarian tribesman, not an artificer to False Gods. Something very strange had happened to the dwarves amid the rubble of Khazduroth.

The dwarf spoke again. "There is blood-debt between us. You saved my life and debts must be balanced," the dwarf said.

"What is your name?" Karnea asked.

"I am Verlek Lastborn," said the dwarf. The humans introduced themselves. The dwarf bowed, without ever taking his eyes off them.

"We came seeking knowledge of the Lost Runes," said Karnea. She revealed her armlet. "If you could tell us where we might find more like this, all debts will be discharged."

"You will not find it here," Verlek said.

"We were told this was found in the Forge Quarter."

"Once perhaps you would have found its like here, but this place has been picked clean of all precious stuff by the goblins and the Shadow worshippers."

"Then our quest is in vain," said Karnea. Her shoulders slumped.

The dwarf's beard rippled oddly. He made a chopping gesture with his hand. "Perhaps not. I am young and not wise. Among the clan I am considered least. There are those who know more than I. Guttri or Ferik or Branhilde the Beautiful may know where to find what you seek. Guttri knows about runes. My mother does too."

"Would they help us?"

"I do not know. Only I have blood-debt to you. Yet I am owed some small debts myself. Perhaps they would aid you if I asked them, in return for cancellation of such. It is worth attempting."

"Where can we find this Guttri?" Kormak asked.

"He dwells within the Hold of the Faithful."

"Will you take us there?"

"I cannot give you permission to enter the Hold, but I can take you to within hailing distance of it and then we shall see what we shall see."

Karnea looked at Kormak. There was a glimmer of hope in her eyes. It seemed like their mission might not be doomed after all.

Kormak shrugged. "We would be grateful for any aid you might render us," he said.

\*\*\*

Verlek led the way deeper into the darkness. There was no hesitation in his manner. He moved with the ease of a man walking through a familiar neighbourhood in his home city. He moved swiftly, on all fours, long arms touching the ground like those of the apes Kormak had seen in southern lands beyond the Dragon Sea. He realised now that this was what the dwarf reminded him of, even down to the facial shape and features. His people seemed more akin to those huge beasts than to men.

The main difference from the apes was the lack of body hair and the beard. Its tendrils rippled constantly. His ears moved slightly as well, tracking around as if intent on finding the source of any sound. Occasionally the dwarf paused and let his beard dangle on the ground between his fingers. He looked then like a man listening carefully.

They moved in his wake, following him down ramps and stairwells, passing more giant statues of Old Ones and massive stone pillars from which strange gurgling sounds emerged, as if water or other fluids were running through their cores.

"Are you sure this is wise?" Sasha asked. The dwarf's ears twitched when she spoke but he never broke stride otherwise. "He could be leading us into a trap."

"We were surrounded by goblins and monsters, anyway," Karnea said. Was there a note of disapproval in her voice of the way Sasha's guidance had led them to this? "At least this way we have a chance of finding what we came for."

"He only said the others might be able to help us," Kormak said. "And dwarves are very precise in their use of language."

"They also pay their debts," said Karnea. "And Verlek feels we saved his life."

"That's because the Guardian did save his life," said Boreas. A grim smile stretched his skull-like features.

"What was that about you carrying a forbidden weapon?" said Sasha.

"I don't know," said Kormak. "The dwarves of Aethelas never said anything about that."

"Marked with runes of Chaos and Death, he said," said Karnea. "Yet if you look, he has a similar rune on his left forearm. The one that looks like a single-eyed octopus, the spell-breaking rune,"

Kormak remembered what Master Malan had once told him. "It disrupts magic the way an Elder Sign does."

"A servant of the Old Ones would not have such an Elder Sign tattooed on his body," said Karnea. "It would be blasphemy to them."

"The dwarves beneath Aethelas don't mind having them emblazoned on the doors of their halls," said Kormak.

"I don't think these dwarves have much in common with your allies. Not any more. If ever they did."

"You think they might be hostile?" Kormak asked.

"The dwarves beneath the Holy Mountain make weapons that can kill Old Ones. Verlek describes himself as one of the Faithful. Maybe they represent different factions. We don't really know much of dwarvish history other than what our allies have told us."

"Which is what?" Sasha said. Karnea and Boreas both glared at her. She looked back unabashed. "I am in this as much as you, and let's face it, even if you tell me some secret, it is likely to die with me."

"We know they fled the City in the Deeps because of what they call the Long Dying," said Karnea eventually. "They were betrayed and cursed by the Old Ones. They agreed to make weapons for the Order of the Dawn in return for the Order's protection when the Guardians discovered their hidden citadel beneath Mount Aethelas."

"When did this happen?"

"More than a thousand years ago in the time of Althuriel, the Sun King," Kormak said. "It was the beginning of a long alliance. They gave us a weapon that let us deal with the Old Ones. One that forced them to respect the Law."

"The swords are so important then?"

"It is supposed to be impossible to kill an Old One without such a blade," said Boreas.

"Not impossible," said Kormak. "Just close to it. They heal almost instantly from normal wounds. Always. They can even come back from death, given sufficient time."

"Some very powerful magics can destroy them," Karnea said. "Elder Signs can bind and burn them. Exposure to sunlight, too."

"There are few magicians who are trusted and the Old Ones avoid fighting through the day," said Kormak. "The Solari had weapons that used the Holy Sun's Light but the secrets of making those were lost when the First Empire fell. All we really have now are the blades. They allowed the Sunlanders to turn back the Selenean Resurgence when the Old Ones sought to reclaim the ancient lands the Solari had taken."

"I can understand why the Old Ones would curse the dwarves and even want them destroyed. If they knew the secret of ending their immortality..." Sasha was quick on the uptake.

"But why would they do that?" Boreas asked. "I had always heard the dwarves were loyal to their masters."

"I don't know," said Karnea. "But it is possible that we might find answers even to that if we can find this Hold of which Verlek speaks." She sounded more excited by that possibility than she had by the possibility of finding the Lost Runes. Her cheerfulness was fast re-exerting itself. Kormak was not sure that was a good sign.

# CHAPTER SEVENTEEN

THEY WALKED FOR a long time. The dwarf loped ahead tirelessly. Karnea went forward to talk to him. "We must rest," she said. "I can barely walk."

"You are weary?" The dwarf sounded surprised. "We have come barely five leagues. It is a long way yet to the Hold."

"Nonetheless we must rest and eat if we are to make the journey. Not all of us are as hardy as dwarves."

"So I can see," said Verlek. His nose twitched. His beard flowed. "There is a well not too far from here and a place we can make secure. Now that we have left the Forge Quarter, the accursed Graghur-spawn may pick up our trail once more.

"Graghur-spawn?" Karnea asked. Verlek described the goblins. He placed more emphasis on their sound and smell than their physical appearance.

"He is their progenitor. Or so Guttri has always said and Guttri knows about these things. Guttri is the Keeper." Verlek spoke the title with some respect and he clearly expected them to understand why.

"You mean Graghur created them?" Karnea asked.

"He is mother and father to them. At least so it is written on his monument."

"There is a statue to him?" Kormak asked.

"We passed it but a half league back between the statues of Saa-Aquor, Mistress of the Seas and Tritureon, High Lord of the Black Swamp Ziggurat," said Verlek. "Surely you perceived it. Carved from star-stone, smelled of it too. The texture was very fine."

"I do not recall seeing such a thing," said Kormak. There had been a statue of a tall stately Old One who looked not unlike a dwarf being borne along on a platform carried by a score of goblins. It came to him then he was making a very elementary mistake.

"Graghur is a shapeshifter," he said.

"All the Eldrim are," said Verlek, as if stating something obvious to a child. "Sometimes they choose to remain in a given form. Sometimes they get stuck in it."

"He could have picked a better shape," said Kormak.

"You have encountered him?" The dwarf's blind-seeming eyes were turned on him.

"Yes."

"And you are alive?"

"Apparently."

"You bear a forbidden blade." Verlek said this as if it held the secret of Kormak's survival, which in a way, it did. The dwarf looked thoughtful then his head twitched to one side and he made a sign over his chest and a cursing sound.

"What?" Kormak asked.

"I was thinking blasphemous thoughts," said Verlek. "I am young and untested and I don't know any better."

It sounded like he was repeating something he had been told often by others. Some of what the dwarf had said earlier came back to

Kormak. "The goblins are your enemies," he said.

Verlek made a curious movement of his head that Kormak was fast coming to equate with a nod of assent.

"Then Graghur is too," said Karnea.

Another head movement. Verlek's beard twitched in an agitated manner. His eyes narrowed. His mouth shut tight as if he was trying to hold in words by force of will.

"We can help you against him," said Karnea. "At least the Guardian can."

"That decision is not mine to make," said Verlek, but there was a note of excitement, almost of hope in his voice that had not been there before. There was something else too, a note of horror, as if he was contemplating something unspeakable.

"I have never seen tattoos like yours before," Karnea said. "They are rune script."

"Yes. They are Branhilde's work and they have helped keep me alive when others have fallen."

"Life in the Underhalls is dangerous," Karnea said. Kormak remained silent. He noticed that Verlek was more likely to reply when she spoke. He was not sure whether it was because she was a female or because she was simply a more sympathetic listener than he was.

"Indeed but I have survived fifty full years," said Verlek. "No one thought I would when I was born."

"Your name, Lastborn, that is quite literally true, is it not? You are the last child to have been born among your people."

"That is truth." Kormak heard talk coming from behind him. Sasha and Boreas, excluded from the conversation here were talking among themselves. They seemed to be getting on. He focused attention back on Verlek.

"That is hard to imagine," said Karnea. "I know few children are born among dwarves but I would have expected more than one birth in fifty years."

The dwarf looked away. In a human, Kormak would have taken his expression for embarrassment. He fell silent. Perhaps he felt he was giving too much away. Kormak decided it was his turn to change the subject.

"You came a long way from your Hold on your own," he said. "What brought you to the Forge Quarter?"

Verlek continued to be silent for a long time as he loped along. Kormak wondered if he was going to get any answer at all.

"I wanted to prove myself against one of the beasts that Graghur unleashes there. Utti questioned my courage and I decided to show him. I told him I would bring back Yellow Eye's head as an ornament for the Wall of Skulls."

"You could have," said Kormak. "Yellow Eye is dead."

"I did not kill him," said Verlek. "I was taken by surprise by the Slitherer while stalking him and would have died had you not come along. There is no honour to be gained taking such a skull. Instead I gained a debt, and perhaps something more." He showed a small smile. "Aye, and perhaps something more."

They walked through the dark corridors in silence. In the distance a drumming sound started. A familiar howling echoed through the corridors.

"The Graghur-spawn have found our trail again," said Verlek. "There can be no rest now."

The howls echoed through the corridors behind them. Verlek loped along easily on all fours. He was not very fast compared to a man sprinting but he had proved he could easily keep up this pace for hours. He was showing not the slightest sign of strain. The same could not be said for Kormak or his companions.

"They are driving us before them," said Verlek. "Some have circled ahead. We are in the jaws of a pincer."

He spoke easily. His breath did not come gasping from his mouth.

Kormak said, "We can turn and fight."

"If worst comes to worst, we shall," said Verlek. "But there are too many of them. At least a hundred goblins, a score of the great goblins and a pack of hunting wolves."

"How can you tell?" Kormak asked.

"Can you not hear them? Smell them? Feel them in your beard." He made a grimace that again suggested embarrassment. "Of course, you have no beard."

Was it possible that Verlek's beard was some sort of sensory organ, like a tongue or a nose? Could he smell things with it, feel them or was it some other sense, unknown to humanity such as those that some of the Old Ones possessed? He remembered the dwarf touching the floor with it previously. Did it pick up vibrations? Now did not seem to be the time to be asking about it.

"Run!" Kormak said.

\*\*\*

They raced through what might have been a long tunnel. Blank windows and doorways gaped on every side. Huge pillars, spaced every fifty strides obscured the view. On each, massive runes had been worked and Kormak felt the pulse of magical energy rushing through them.

The howling of the wolves was louder now. Mingled with it he could hear the high-pitched squeaking yelps of goblins.

"Run faster," said Verlek. "We are almost at the Hold. If we can reach it, there is chance we might escape."

Kormak did not ask any questions. The dwarf had lengthened his stride and was moving faster now. Under normal circumstances Kormak would not have had much difficulty keeping up but he was tired. A glance behind him told him that the others were no better off. In fact, Karnea looked as if she was on the verge of collapse. Her face was completely red. Her hair was lank and sweat ran down her brow. Even Boreas looked weary.

Ahead of them now, he could see another bridge; a long structure of fused stone, lined by enormous statues of what might have been dwarf heroes or might have been Old Ones. It was too dark too tell.

Kormak dropped back. Karnea stood there, blowing air from her lips, clutching her side. "A stitch," she said. "I can't go on. Run! Save yourselves."

"We're not leaving without you," Kormak said. He grinned encouragingly.

She gulped and swallowed and leaned forward, bracing her hands on her knees. Behind them, Kormak thought he saw dark shapes moving through the tunnel. The howls were amplified by the tunnel mouth.

Boreas handed Kormak his hammer and swept Karnea up. "I will carry her," he said. He was as good as his word. He held the scholar like she was nothing more than a child. Verlek turned and reached out for the hammer himself. Kormak let him have it. The dwarf carried the weapon as easily one handed as Boreas had with two but he was slowed down because he could no longer run on all fours.

"I owe you my life," he said. "Debts must be paid. Get to the bridge."

"Don't be foolish," said Kormak. "Your own people might kill us, if you are not there to speak for us."

A spark of what might have been anger appeared in the dwarf's eye. He raised the hammer as if testing its weight for a swing. "You are right," he said. "We have other hammers. I will gift your companion with one in return for losing this."

He dropped the hammer and loped off in the direction of the bridge. Kormak risked a look around. He could see that the others had almost reached it. White wolves were starting to be visible in the greenish glow. He turned and sprinted after the dwarf. Every breath burned in his chest.

\*\*\*

They raced across the bridge. Each of the shadowy figures had an everglow lantern mounted on it. The light was dim compared even to moonlight but, after the long darkness they had wandered through, now seemed like daylight to Kormak's eyes. All of the huge figures appeared to be dwarves, he noticed, but how could he be certain. Perhaps they were shape-shifted Old Ones like Graghur.

Once they were on the far side Verlek took the horn from around his neck and sounded it. Its blast, uncannily loud, echoed away into the gloom, for a moment even drowning out the howling of the wolves.

A glance over his shoulder showed Kormak that, just for a moment, the pursuing beasts had halted. Perhaps they feared the onset of some enemy. They waited for heartbeats only though before taking up the chase once more.

Kormak could see the great goblins. They looked like their smaller kin, but tall as a man and skinnier, as if someone had taken an extraordinarily large goblin and stretched it on a rack. One of them carried a banner showing a goblin head with four stylised arms radiating out from it. The others brandished huge curved blades and oval shields with grinning skull faces inscribed on them.

Ahead lay a huge lit courtyard, surrounded on three sides by massive fortified walls. In the centre of the wall directly ahead was a massive stone doorway, inscribed with powerful warding runes.

Verlek sounded his horn desperately. Shadowy shapes moved on the balconies of the fortification above them.

A howl came from very close behind Kormak. He turned. A dire wolf snapped at him. Its goblin rider thrust with its spear. Kormak parried it, beheaded the wolf, and then stabbed the rider through the chest even as he tumbled to the ground.

The other dire wolves were almost upon him, and behind them came a company of tall, thin great goblins with wicked looking blades.

The first of the mangy dire wolves sprang. Kormak stepped to one side, letting the wolf pass through the empty air where he had been. It landed, twisted immediately, snapped at him with jaws that could tear off an arm. He leapt back as another wolf attacked him.

The pack surrounded him. Red eyes glittered with insane ferocity. Froth bubbled over yellow fangs and lolling pink tongues.

He slashed the throat of the nearest dire wolf. Blood spurted, spraying Kormak and the ground at his feet. The red fluid tasted metallic on his tongue.

Two wolves attacked, one from each side. He avoided the first but the second snagged the sleeve of his jerkin and pulled him off balance.

He snapped the pommel of his blade down on the wolf's sensitive nose, and it released its grip on him, whimpering in pain. The second wolf sprang at him. He did not have time to get his blade into position. It overbore him, its massive weight pressing his body to the ground, huge jaws snapping down towards his throat.

An eerie whistling sound filled the air and a moment later an explosion of infernal brightness burst overhead, distracting the wolf.

Kormak rolled, knocking it off balance. Clumsily he swung his sword round and down, connecting with the wolf's skull, splitting it. The wolf reared, blood pouring down into its eyes, brains spilling from the gash in its head. Kormak rolled against its back legs, his weight knocking it over. As he rose to his feet he saw that it was dead. It had just taken a few moments to realise it.

A quick glance showed him that all was confusion. The goblin horde had raced into the plaza behind the wolves. The great goblins were in the lead but scores and scores of the smaller creatures scurried in their wake. Comet trails of fire descended from the balconies on either side of the plaza and where they touched the ground, huge explosions ripped the darkness. A wave of heat washed over them and then vanished. The rune on Karnea's arm blazed brightly as it fed on the energy.

It only took Kormak a moment to realise that the defenders were using larger versions of Sasha's weapon. The goblins yipped and screamed but kept coming, too filled with the thrill of pursuit to consider flight. Their prey was in sight and they were not going to let it escape.

The great goblins closed with Kormak. In the light of the explosions, he made out their lean horrible faces leering at him. Mouths full of razor sharp teeth grinned evilly. They emitted strange chirping sounds and their huge bat-like ears twisted as if in response heartbeats later. In the flickering light of the exploding runestones, their eyes changed colour in response to the intensity of the flames, going from very dark to almost glitteringly light as the explosions burst and faded.

Kormak picked the closest group and sprang towards it, lashing out with his blade, cutting armour and flesh as if it were cloth, shattering bone as easily if it were porcelain. Within a dozen heartbeats, half a dozen of the great goblins were dead and he was carving a way through their line.

His instincts told him not to go too far. Doing so would take him into the line of fire for the exploding runestones and no blade could protect him from those. He needed to be close to Karnea and Sasha if he was going to protect them too.

A horn sounded close to him and turning he saw that Verlek and Boreas had returned to fight beside him. The dwarf's axe flickered around him almost too fast for the eye to follow. Boreas had picked up a goblin scimitar. A glance behind him showed that Karnea stood near one of the great doors, Sasha beside her with a dagger in each hand.

All around them the goblin army surged, a sea of scaled flesh assaulting an island of whirling steel. Kormak cut and parried and slashed, losing track of everything in his desperate fury. Standing alone, any of the three would have been cut down at once but forming a triangle, and watching each other's backs they managed to withstand the onslaught.

Kormak knew it was only a matter of time before the end came. Soon they would become too weary to parry their foes, or a lucky blow would get through and take one of them down, and then it would all be over.

He redoubled his efforts to slay, knowing that there was no hope of survival, determined that he was going to drag as many of his enemies down into death with him as he could. The unleashed fury of his blade was too much for the goblins. He drove them back towards the bridge, moving further from the gate. Howling desperate war-cries, Verlek and Boreas accompanied him.

The hail of runestones stopped. That was it then. His last hope, that the goblins would break in the face of the unrelenting hail of explosive missiles, died. They were on their own now and it was only a matter of time before they were pulled down.

# CHAPTER EIGHTEEN

A STRANGE MOMENT of calm swept over the battlefield. For a moment, the goblin assault ceased and all the screams and clamour faded away.

He stood amid a pile of fallen bodies, bleeding from scores of small cuts, and surveyed the sea of goblin faces. They had killed dozens but it made no difference, hundreds more waited to cut them down. They were encircled by the goblins, hundreds of saucer eyes stared at them. The creatures seemed to smile, revealing rows and rows of small sharp teeth and then, as if at a prearranged signal, began to chant the name of Graghur.

Horns sounded behind them. There was a grinding sound as if a great stone gate was being opened. The sounds of dwarf battle-cries rang across the plaza with the clangour of weapon upon weapon.

"Ferik has sallied forth," Verlek shouted in Kormak's ear. There was something like pure, unrestrained joy in his voice. The dwarf seemed drunk on killing. "I knew he would not be able to resist joining in such a fray!"

Much good that will do us, Kormak thought, unless we can join him. A quick glance back over his shoulder showed him that a flying wedge of heavily armed dwarves charging the goblin forces. "Back!" he shouted and began to cut a path through towards their rescuers. Boreas and Verlek followed.

The dwarves smashed through the confused goblins like the prow of a ship breaking through a wave. They left piles of dead and broken bodies around them. All of the dwarves were half-naked and made savage by their runic tattoos. Some of those glowed in the darkness as if focusing magical powers. The male dwarves were for the most part broader and more muscular even than Verlek, with longer beards that swirled around them as they fought. The females were just as underdressed and just as tattooed and they fought alongside the males with even greater fury.

Their chanting had taken on a resemblance to some great, strange song, like that of the galley slaves Kormak had once served among as they rowed. The dwarves moved in time to the chant, struck their blows on its beats. Their song seemed to bind them into one mighty, multi-limbed organism.

Comet trails descended from the walls again, explosions tore the further points of the goblin lines. Under the sheer force of the dwarven attack, their pursuers turned tail and fled, leaving Kormak and his companions to confront the angry, uncomprehending glares of the dwarves across the blood-soaked paving stones of the battlefield.

The tide of goblins flowed back across the bridge, scuttling as fast as their legs could carry them, the few surviving wolves leading the retreat. The dwarves chased them down, slaughtering those they caught. Some of the dwarves were going around the battlefield, severing goblin heads and collecting them. Bones splintered and spines snapped as they did so.

Kormak found himself confronting the largest dwarf he had seen so far. This one came almost to his throat and was far broader than Verlek, seeming almost as wide as he was tall. His tattooed arms were like tree-trunks and he held a great pick in one hand and an axe in the other. His beard reached almost to the ground even when he stood straight and it rippled like a nest of snakes. The dwarf's ears twitched and his blank-seeming gaze met Kormak's levelly.

"I knew you would not be able to resist such a fight, Ferik sire," said Verlek happily. He seemed mightily pleased with himself, as if he had sprung a surprise party purely for the benefit of this huge dwarf champion. The massive dwarf bent over and severed a goblin head with a short savage chop of his axe. He did not once take his eyes off Kormak.

"You have caused a lot of trouble, youngling," said Ferik. There was an undertone of exasperated affection as well as controlled anger in his tone. "What new trouble have you brought on the Hold now?"

Ferik's eyes were fixed on Kormak's blade. His beard rippled towards the Guardian, as if reaching out in his direction. Kormak sensed the tremendous power in this dwarf and the explosive violence. He realised it would not take too much to have it directed at him.

"I have blood-debt to these men," said Verlek.

"You have blood-debt to Shadow worshipers?" The anger in that great booming voice outweighed the affection. There was suspicion in Ferik's expression now. He tilted his head to one side as he examined the younger dwarf.

"I am not a Shadow worshipper," said Kormak. "I am a champion of the Holy Sun."

The strange dark eyes turned to regard Kormak. The lips tightened, revealing tombstone teeth in a mirthless grin. "You will speak when spoken to, man, or you will die. I am having words with my son. When I am done, I will have words for you."

Kormak took a tight rein on his own anger. He was not used to being talked to in such a fashion but he was surrounded by the dwarves and he needed their help.

"He slew the Slitherer, father," said Verlek. "He has killed many goblins. You have seen it with your own eyes. He can take many skulls."

"The followers of the Shadow are cunning and given to many deceptions," said another dwarf from nearby. He was not as large as Ferik and his face was leaner. There was something about the set of his mouth that did not seem quite right, that gave his face a sneering look. Kormak could see that this dwarf had a severed goblin head in each hand. He was holding them by their ears.

"My life is beholden to them, Utti," said Verlek. "I have talked with them. I say they are not followers of the Shadow."

Utti turned his sneering face to Verlek. "And what would one so young know about the ways of the Shadow? You have barely grown a beard, boy."

The air between them fairly crackled with tension. There seemed to be real hostility between these two, Kormak thought.

"Aye, Utti, but I know how to fight, unlike some, who collect heads of those they did not kill for the Wall of Skulls."

Kormak saw that all of the dwarves were red-handed now and were piling up small mounds of severed heads in front of them. Boreas was watching all of this with narrowed eyes. He did not understand Dwarvish but he could hear that the tone of speech was not friendly. Kormak put a hand on Boreas' arm just to let him know everything was all right.

"There are four more heads we could take right here," said Utti.

He turned to look at Kormak once more. Kormak met his stare levelly. He did not want trouble but if he was attacked he would respond. Utti's beard twisted and writhed and seemed to be tangling its furthest end in knots. He took a step back almost as if he had been reading Kormak's mind. Ferik laughed. It was a sound like stone grating against stone.

"Utti has just discovered that taking this one's head might be harder than he thought." Kormak sensed a change in the air. There was still suspicion and hostility but there was no longer a sense of imminent violence coming from Ferik. He realised the change had happened during the exchange between Utti and Verlek and just afterwards. Was it possible that Ferik did not like Utti?

Utti spat on the ground, but carefully. The spittle did not land anywhere near Kormak or the other dwarves. Ferik glanced around. It seemed like all the heads had been taken. The dwarves were starting to place them within sacks. They looked as happy as children who had collected their gifts on a feastday morning.

"We do not need to decide to do what to do with these humans right now," said Ferik. He turned and looked at Kormak. "Put down your weapons!" he said.

Kormak looked back at him. Every fibre of his being rebelled against putting down his sword. He would almost rather lay down his life.

Ferik sensed this. Suddenly the violence was back in the air.

"You have the look of a handy man with a blade, whatever else you may be," said the dwarf. "But we outnumber you and be assured we will kill you if you do not do as you are told."

There was utter confidence in the dwarf's manner. Kormak considered the situation. He could hold onto the sword and die. In that case, he would still have lost the blade. At least if he was still alive he might be able to reclaim it.

"Be not afraid, that anyone will take your sword. No one would want to carry such an unholy weapon," said Ferik.

"The sword was forged by dwarves," said Kormak.

"Aye, to our shame it was," said the dwarf.

"I will carry it until it may be returned to you," said Verlek. He said this as if he were taking a great burden upon himself. Kormak felt sure this was not from the responsibility of holding the weapon but because of the nature of the thing he had to carry. He seemed embarrassed but determined to do this anyway. He held out one huge hand to Kormak.

Kormak still considered refusing. He could see the tension in Ferik now. He glanced around and the other dwarves were all staring at him. One or two were thumbing the blades of their axes. The prospect of taking another skull seemed to appeal to them.

Abruptly, he pushed the scabbarded blade into the young dwarf's hand. "Take good care of it," he said.

"I will do my best," said Verlek.

He slung it over his back as he had seen Kormak do. The Guardian wondered if he had made a huge mistake as the dwarves crowded in around him.

***

All of the humans were stripped of any weapons they were carrying. They took away Karnea's bag of adjuncts and the rune on her arm as well. They seemed familiar with power of such things.

The dwarves looked oddly at Sasha when they took away her runestone thrower. One or two of them grumbled to each other in a tone that suggested that some dark suspicion had been confirmed.

"What is going on?" she asked.

"We are being held prisoner," said Kormak. "Until they decide what to do with us."

"They don't look any too friendly," said Boreas. He went to stand beside Sasha, and hovered by her protectively.

"They think we are Shadow worshippers," said Kormak. "I suspect they think everyone who lives outside their walls is one."

"Living in this place I can see how they would believe that," said Karnea.

Utti leaned forward and said very softly, "Be silent. Speak when you are told to."

Karnea flinched away from him. Kormak stepped between the dwarf and the scholar. Utti did not seem quite so intimidated now that he was the only one of the two of them holding a weapon.

They were led into a vast hall with many low arched openings leading off from it. The guards took them to the right and led them down a long ramp. There were faint lights here glowing in the ceiling. They appeared to be of the same type as the one Karnea had carried and which had now been confiscated.

At the end of a corridor they were pushed through an arch. After they were inside a massive stone door slid down from the top of the arch, effectively cutting them off from all escape. Kormak looked around. The walls of the room were bare. There was no furniture. The place was more barren than any cell he had ever been in.

Sasha spread her hands wide and gave them a wan smile. "Just when I think things can't get worse, they somehow manage to," she said.

"We're still alive," said Kormak.

"There's a lot of dwarves out there who seem to wish we were otherwise," said Boreas.

"I don't think their leaders want us dead."

"Was the big one with the long beard their leader then?"

"Warleader perhaps. I don't know if he was their chief."

"Bastards took my stonethrower," said Sasha.

"They think you stole it," Karnea said. "I heard one of them say so."

"How could I have stolen it from them? I've never set eyes on one of them before this trip."

"I think they regard everything down here as their property. Not without reason since their ancestors made it."

"You always seem to take their side," said Sasha.

"There are no sides here," said Karnea. "We should all be on the same side."

"The dwarves don't seem to think so," Kormak said. Sasha looked at him gratefully. "They regard my sword as some sort of forbidden weapon, a device of evil. How could that be? It was made by dwarves."

Karnea looked at him sidelong and Kormak felt suddenly naive. It was not a sensation he was used to. "How many men do you know who claim the works of other men are evil? There can be differences of opinions between dwarves as well as humans. It's hardly surprising given the differences between these dwarves and those beneath Aethelas."

"Differences?" Kormak asked.

"You have never encountered those dwarves, Sir Kormak? I am surprised."

"I have been below, but they did not allow me to see them."

"No. They would not. I did not see my first dwarf until I had been below for six months. They do not willingly deal with us face to face."

"How are the two tribes different?" Sasha asked. She looked genuinely curious.

"These ones are much more primitive. They dress like orcs or southern barbarians, which is to say hardly at all. Their speech is rough and their runework, at least as exemplified by their tattoos, is both crudely done and over-elaborate."

"You are saying these ones are less civilised?"

"Less sophisticated certainly."

"They are the ones who remained in the City in the Deeps. You would think it would be the opposite."

"A lot of things can happen in two thousand years."

"I agree with you," said Sasha. "They are certainly not what I expected, judging from the statues and artefacts we found in the Underhalls. These are like Aquilean hill-tribesmen. They don't seem much above the level of goblins themselves."

"Something happened here," said Karnea. "And I mean to find out what if it kills me."

"I don't think it's the finding out that will kill you," said Kormak. "It will most likely be a dwarven axe."

As he said the words, there was a creaking sound and the door slid slowly upwards. Two armed dwarves blocked the exit. Others stood behind them.

# CHAPTER NINETEEN

THE TWO ARMED dwarves entered. One of them was Utti, who gave them an evil look. The other was a hulking brute who Kormak did not recognise but who seemed to take his cue from Utti. They pushed the humans back against the far wall. Verlek entered bearing a tray of food and drink. He eyed the chamber with distaste then set the tray down on the floor.

Two of the dwarves retreated outside. Verlek and Utti remained as the door slid down. "Eat!" said Verlek. Kormak moved forward and inspected the plates. They contained slabs of something cooked in a very black sauce. There was flask and four small stone goblets as well. Kormak took one of the plates and a spoon and took a small taste of the slab. It was a mushroom in some sort of fermented sauce. The taste was not as unpleasant as he had expected.

"We won't poison you," said Utti. He sounded as if he had given the subject some consideration though. Kormak got the impression Utti would not mind poisoning them if he could get away with it. He poured some of the dark liquid into a flask and sipped it. It burned going down his throat and he had to fight to keep from spluttering. It was definitely very, very alcoholic. Kormak indicated that the others should eat and they fell too with a will. He realised it was a very long time since they had eaten.

"Not a place I would have put guests," said Verlek. "It is an old storechamber."

"They are not our guests," said Utti.

"They are not our enemies either," said Verlek.

"Not until the Dwarfmoot decides so."

"The Dwarfmoot may decide they are our allies," said Verlek.

"I doubt it," said Utti. "There are the Faithful and there is everyone else."

"Why do you call yourselves the Faithful?" Karnea asked.

Utti looked at the ceiling and blew air out through his lips with a peculiar fluttering sound. His beard fluttered around, its ends tying themselves into knots.

"We call ourselves that because we kept the faith," said Verlek.

"When others did not?" Karnea asked.

Verlek nodded.

"Other dwarves?" Karnea prompted.

"Yes," said Verlek. He was looking away. His beard writhed now as well. Did that signify embarrassment, Kormak wondered.

"Others broke their oaths," said Utti suddenly. There was a boastful tone in his voice. "We did not."

"Do you refer to the ones who forged my sword?" Kormak asked.

"They made that which it was forbidden to make," said Utti. "They marked their blades with the runes of Chaos and Death. They made that which was forbidden by our mistress, by all of the Eldrim."

"Not all," said Verlek. Utti glared at him. His beard went rigid and stopped moving altogether.

"Stare all you like," said Verlek. "But you know I have truth. The

Exiles did what they did at the behest of Eldrim."

"So they claimed," said Utti. He sounded as if he did not believe that was the case. Karnea chewed her lips as they talked. She desperately wanted them to keep talking so much was obvious. She did not dare interrupt them even to ask a question. "These are not matters to be spoken on before outsiders."

Verlek shrugged. "I have questions of my own to put to you, if you would answer them."

Karnea nodded eagerly. Utti felt compelled to say, "If you do not answer them willingly, you will answer them later with your hand in the furnace."

"I will answer any questions you have truthfully and honestly unless they go against oaths I have spoken," said Karnea. "And if they do, I will tell you."

"Fairly spoken," Verlek said. Utti merely grunted. "Where do you come from?"

"We come from the surface," said Karnea. "From beyond the City in the Deeps."

"You dwell among the monsters and Shadow worshippers?"

"We dwell among men."

"So you serve those who opposed the Eldrim."

"We serve the Holy Sun," Karnea said. "We oppose the Old Ones only when they break the Law."

"Who makes a Law that binds the Eldrim?" Utti sneered.

"The Old Ones did," said Kormak. "They agreed to it with our masters and the kings of men. It has kept peace between us for a thousand years."

"You lie," said Utti. "The Eldrim would not negotiate with their inferiors."

"They are intelligent," said Kormak. "They will negotiate with anyone who has the power to destroy them."

"And you claim you do?"

"You already know the answer to that," said Kormak. "You have seen the sword. You know what it does. There are hundreds more like it."

"An obscenity," said Utti.

"Why do you say that?" Karnea asked.

Utti did not answer. Karnea continued patiently as if Utti had not interrupted her. She seemed to take real pleasure in explaining things. "We come from the surface. We guess you have not had much contact with it since the city was sealed."

"We have all we need here," said Verlek. "And we have our duty to perform. We would not desert our post. We keep the faith." Again he said this as if he were talking about matters of the utmost importance. What could have kept the dwarves here in a city wracked by plague and all but abandoned?

"Things have changed since the days of glory though," said Karnea. "Your people have changed."

Verlek made the dwarven equivalent of a nod, a little sadly, it seemed. "Much has been forgotten. Much has been lost. The people are slowly dying."

Utti glared at him once more. "You talk too much."

"I speak only truth."

"It has gotten much worse since Graghur returned, has it not?" Kormak asked. He was guessing but he thought he would throw that out just to see what kind of response it got.

Verlek nodded. "That is so. He is powerful and he is wicked and he seeks to destroy that which we protect."

"He is an Old One," said Kormak. He looked at Utti. "Do you revere him?"

Utti looked away. He made a peculiar grimace that Kormak could not interpret. Verlek spoke. He was clearly uncomfortable with the idea of opposing an Old One.

"He has his own shrine," Verlek said. "You have seen his statue in the Underhalls."

Utti rose and gestured to Verlek. "We are done talking."

Verlek looked as if he wanted to defy Utti but he did not. Utti placed his hand on the door and drummed his fingers in a delicate pattern. With a creaking noise, the doorway rose again and the dwarves left.

Karnea stared at Kormak. "There is much that is strange here."

"What were they saying?" Boreas asked. Karnea explained the gist of it to them, while Kormak studied the door. He wondered whether it had opened in response to the pattern Utti had tapped or whether that had been merely a signal for those outside to open it.

"You are saying that they revere the Old Ones. They think Kormak's weapon is a blasphemy and yet they are forced to fight against Graghur."

"It is a fight they cannot win, if they do not use the right weapon," said Kormak.

"Let's hope they know that too," said Boreas.

***

The storehouse clearly had not been intended to hold living things. The air was close and stale and Kormak found himself wondering if they would suffocate if they remained trapped here too long. They lay on the flagstones and tried to sleep. There was little else for them to do save talk in subdued tones and that had swiftly become depressing.

Kormak stared at the ceiling and tried to plan a method of escape. They could try and overpower the guards when next the cell was opened, but even if they succeeded what then? They were still within the dwarf fortress and surrounded by an undetermined number of the Khazduri. Should they manage to escape, they needed to retrace their steps through the vast goblin haunted maze of the City in the Deeps. And they still would not have found what they came for.

They needed to convince the dwarves not to kill them, and to help them. It was not going to be easy since in the eyes of the dwarves they were heretics and blasphemers. He thought about that. It went against all the things he had been taught about the dwarves since he was a boy. They had rebelled against the Old Ones, just like many of the other Servitor Races. They hated their former masters with a passion. That was why they had created the runeswords for the Order. They were allies of men. Yet the dwarves they had found here did not fit that pattern. They still revered the Old Ones even though one of their ancient masters seemed hell-bent on destroying them.

He pushed all of these thoughts to one side. None of them were helping and none of them made the slightest difference. He needed to find out more. He needed to get out of this prison. He needed to get his sword back. He felt almost naked without it and he experienced a deep sense of shame when he remembered how he had surrendered it. He knew he was going to have to do something to expunge that.

Eventually, sleep came.

***

The door slid open with a grinding creak. Verlek, Utti and a number of other heavily armed dwarf warriors were there. Only Verlek looked remotely friendly and even his beard twisted agitatedly.

"You are to come with us, strangers," said Utti. In Dwarvish,

Kormak remembered the word stranger and enemy were synonymous. It seemed somehow appropriate. "The Dwarfmoot will judge you before the Wall of Skulls."

There was a formal note to his speech that masked his dislike, but Kormak sensed some satisfaction in Utti's manner that made him suspect that things were not going to go well for the humans.

The others picked themselves up. All of them looked dirty and dishevelled. It was clear they had not slept well. Utti gestured towards the door. The humans slowly made their way into the corridor. The dwarves fell into position in front and behind them and they marched back through the Hold.

This time their route took them much further and they emerged into a massive hall. A fire blazed before them, the first Kormak could recall seeing in Khazduroth. It emerged from a huge pit in the floor and it was not fuelled by coal or wood. He guessed it was volcanic in origin or perhaps fuelled by gas. Around the flame rose three stone rings, each higher than the next, they formed broad steps leading up to the flame.

By the light of the dancing flames he could see how the Wall of Skulls got its name. The hall was hundreds of strides long. Skulls were piled on top of skulls all the way to the ceiling on every wall. There were thousands of them. He could tell by the position of the scaffolding that behind the first layer of skulls were others. It seemed as if a new wall was being built in front of the old one. He could imagine dozens of layers of skulls running back all the way to the stone walls. Even as he watched, a dwarf on the scaffolding was mortaring more goblin skulls into place.

"The skulls belong to our enemies," said Verlek. Kormak was going to say that he had guessed that but he kept his mouth shut. The young dwarf was the closest thing they had to an ally here and he did not want to alienate him.

"There must be thousands of them," said Karnea.

"Tens of thousands," said Verlek proudly, "dating all the way back to Time of Dying. We have killed many foes. Graghur claims to be the Taker of Skulls but we have done far better. We have beaten his people at their own game." To Kormak it seemed like the dwarves had simply turned themselves into mirrors of their enemy. They had lost themselves in the war and that was a form of defeat.

Around a hundred dwarves were gathered around the fire. All heads turned as the group entered. Beards on the males and hair on the females writhed furiously at the sight of the newcomers. Ferik stood on a stepped dais beside the flame. Above him on an even higher step, stood two more dwarves, one male, one female whom Kormak assumed were the clan leaders.

"All the clan has assembled," said Verlek. Kormak felt a shock. The Hold they had marched through looked as if it had been built for thousands. All those present looked as if they could fit into one or two of its smaller rooms. It came to him then that if this was every member of the clan, then the dwarves of Khazduroth truly were a dying people.

"And now your fate will be sealed," said Utti. There was malice in his voice.

The clan parted to allow the prisoners to be brought before the flame. Kormak found himself looking up at the dwarves on the steps. He noticed that Ferik had a silver chain around his neck marked with ancient dwarf runes. The two he thought of as chieftains wore gold torcs and necklaces marked with runes of mastery. He recognised those. The heat from the flames was making him sweat but the dwarves gave no sign of discomfort.

Ferik raised one massive hand. "Strangers, you have been brought before the assembled people of the Hold to be judged according to the ancient laws of our people. You are interlopers here. You have trespassed on sacred ground. The penalty for your transgressions is death."

# CHAPTER TWENTY

"ARE THERE ANY here who would speak for these strangers," Ferik asked.

Verlek stepped forward. "I would."

"Then stand before the flame and speak." Verlek strode up to the steps and took a position just below Ferik on the lowest step. He turned to face the clan, touched his beard, placed a hand over his heart and bowed.

"I owe these strangers blood-debt," Verlek said. He sounded apologetic about that. "They saved me from the Slitherer and Yellow Eye, leaving both for dead."

That was a nice, hair-splitting touch, Kormak thought. Anyone who had not been there might have taken that as meaning that Kormak and his companions had killed both monsters. "They warded me through the Underhalls, protecting me to the very gates of the Hold even though the goblins were at their heels. It would be a betrayal of their trust to put them to the stranger-death. They have done nothing but good for me, and our people."

Utti made a hissing sound. Verlek continued, his voice gathering strength as he spoke. "They stood with us when the goblins were at

168 | WILLIAM KING

our gate. The one known as Kormak gave us more than twenty skulls for the Wall."

Ferik placed a hand upon his shoulder. "The skulls have not been placed there. They may never be."

Verlek turned and looked up at him. His beard twisted agitatedly. His pointed ears stood erect. Kormak was reminded of an angry cat. "Are the goblins no longer our enemies?"

"If a goblin kills a goblin do we place the dead one's skull in the Wall?" This came from the female dwarf on the highest stone ring. "Only one of the People may place a skull in the wall, for the glory of his ancestors."

"Branhilde the Beautiful speaks truth," said the older male. He glared down at them. His face was stern and looked as if it had been carved from rock. His beard was very white and still. It was quite the longest in the room, reaching all the way to the floor. "Anything else would be in violation of our ancient customs."

"As you say, Guttri. I bow before your wisdom," said Verlek. Suiting action to words he did so. A ripple of laughter, not mocking, quite sympathetic, passed through the assembled crowd. There was a touch of formality and respect to Verlek's action that had pleased the crowd. Kormak sensed a slight relaxation in the tension although he could not tell whether that was caused by Verlek's action or by Guttri putting the young dwarf in his place.

Verlek turned back to face the crowd. "These people could be our allies," he said. "They are mighty warriors and they possess great knowledge of the outside world."

"What need have we of such knowledge," shouted Utti. "We dwell in the City in the Deeps. Everything beyond her gates is a waste full of demons and Shadow worshippers and enemies. So it has been since the

Time of Dying when the city was sealed."

"Utti," said Ferik, holding his hand up in what might have been a warning gesture.

"Not so. They have spoken with our kin."

"Lies!" shouted Utti.

"Utti, you will have your chance to speak, if you so desire," said Ferik. "Now Verlek holds the third step. Now it is his turn to speak."

Utti's ears lost some of their outraged rigour, his beard drooped. "I will hold my peace."

"Good," said Ferik. "Now Verlek, pray continue."

"They claim to have spoken with our kin," said Verlek, speaking slowly and as if he wanted to state everything with complete accuracy. "At very least the truth of these claims must be weighed and tested before there can be any talk of killing these strangers. And I would say should their claims prove to be true, we would do well to listen and aid them as they might aid us against our enemies."

With that, Verlek stepped down from the stone ring and stepped back into the crowd. Kormak saw one or two of the dwarves reach out and slap him affectionately on the back.

"Now is your chance to speak Utti," said Ferik. "If you still desire to."

Utti walked slowly forward, head downcast, clearly considering his words. The flames danced. Thousands of empty eye-sockets stared down menacingly. It seemed as if legions of the dead watched in judgement. Utti stood looking into the flames for a while, back towards the audience, letting curiosity and tension build. After long heartbeats, he bowed to the others on the steps, and turned to the crowd.

"These strangers came here—we do not know why. They claim to come from the surface world—we do not know where. They appear to have helped Verlek—we do not know their reasons." He spoke slowly and in a considered manner. His voice was deep and resonant, and compared to him Verlek had sounded like a child.

"If they were spies, they could not have found a better way of infiltrating our hold, taking advantage of the naive and trusting nature of a young dwarf who does not know any better." The crowd murmured. He raised a hand and said, "I am not saying that is what happened. Let us be fair. I am merely suggesting an explanation of events."

Kormak wondered what trap Utti was about to spring. He felt certain he was going to. He would not have abandoned his obvious but effective line of attack otherwise.

"We live in dark times. Khazduroth is fallen almost to ruin. The old seals have been broken. Shadow worshippers have come here to plunder its treasures. Graghur and his spawn assail us. Our numbers grow too few to protect our sacred trust. Verlek holds out the possibility of alliance with these oh so convenient strangers. He forgets the long history of betrayals and treachery that our people have suffered. He is young. He is impressed by tales that these strangers have spoken with our lost kindred.

"Perhaps he forgets why those kindred were lost to us. Perhaps he forgets the ancient betrayal of our people, the bitter, fratricidal war that sprang up between our kin. Perhaps to him these are only old stories. Perhaps he no longer has faith in our chronicles."

"That is not so!" Verlek shouted. Utti turned and looked ironically at Ferik. Ferik said, "You have had your turn to speak Verlek. Now it is Utti's."

Utti smiled. Now the knife was going to go in, Kormak thought.

The smile widened slowly. Utti looked at the floor again, as if considering his words. All was silent except for the hissing of the dancing flames. All around, every dwarf strained to hear what Utti was going to say.

"I must apologise to Verlek. I spoke without due thought earlier. I sounded as if I was trying to cast doubt on the claims he has made on these strangers behalf. I did not mean to. I believe some of them to be true. It is certainly possible that they have spoken to our treacherous kin. Why do I say this?"

Again he paused. Kormak found that even he was leaning forward, waiting to hear what the dwarf was going to say. Utti raised his hand, palm outwards and then brought it down in a sweeping gesture. His outstretched finger pointed directly at Kormak. "I say it because they came here—here!—bearing one of the forbidden weapons. They have carried an abomination here—here!—onto our sacred ground, into the most holy place of the People of Stone."

There was a collective hiss of indrawn breath. Utti stopped again and Kormak was aware that all eyes in the place were looking at him and every gaze expressed hostility, outrage and anger.

The dwarves turned and moved menacingly towards Kormak. He balled his fists, regretting that he had no more effective weapon and prepared to do what he could. Sasha put some distance between them. Boreas moved to assist him. Karnea looked around blinking out from behind her glasses as if not entirely sure about what was going on.

Ferik bellowed for them to halt. "No decision has been come to yet. If these strangers are to be killed, let it be done according to the Laws of our people."

The dwarves stopped moving towards Kormak but they still eyed him menacingly. Still, Ferik's words had given him some hope. Why would he even mention the word if there was not some chance of them being allowed to remain alive?

"I would hear what these strangers have to say for themselves," said Branhilde the Beautiful.

"That is not usual," said Utti.

"Nonetheless, there is precedent," said Ferik. Branhilde nodded. "In ancient times, allies and outlanders were allowed to speak before the Moot on matters of importance."

"Allies," said Utti. "And that was before the Dying. Those were more trusting times."

"Is there precedent or not?" Verlek asked. Was there a note of mockery in his tone? Utti glared at him and then looked at Branhilde. If he had been a man, Kormak would have thought he was licking his lips.

"There is precedent," said Utti. "Let the stranger speak. I would hear from his own lips why he came here bearing such a forbidden weapon."

"Kormak Swordbearer, you are called to speak, if you so desire."

Kormak strode up out of the crowd and leapt onto the lowest step. He heard some gasps at his effrontery from the assembled dwarves. He felt the blazing heat of the fire behind his back. He felt sweat beading his skin.

"I came here on a mission for my order," he said, speaking slowly and clearly so that he might be understood by all. "I came here as a guard for the scholar, Karnea. We came to the City in the Deeps seeking knowledge of the Lost Runes and the metal netherium. We had hoped to find it or trade for it."

"Why do you seek netherium?" someone in the crowd asked. Kormak could not but suspect that he already knew the answer.

"We seek it in order that we may repair our blades and protect ourselves from the Old Ones," he said. He saw no point in trying to deceive them and he thought he might as well get the worst of it, from the point of view of the dwarves, out into the open at once.

They were staring at him now. He could not help but notice that all of their eyes were pools of blackness. Ferik's had not been, nor Branhilde's nor any of the speakers from the steps. Was it something to do with staring at the flames, he wondered, then realised that was not relevant to what he had to say.

"You admit then that you use your blade to slay Eldrim," said Utti.

"Aye, I have slain the Old Ones but only when they broke the Laws that they agreed to be bound by, just as my people did."

"Blasphemy," someone in the crowd shouted.

"Perhaps for you but not for me," Kormak stated defiantly.

Guttri held up his hand. "I have never heard of such laws."

"They were agreed in the time after the City in the Deeps was sealed."

"So you say."

"I am a Guardian of the Order of the Dawn and I speak the truth in this matter," said Kormak. "And it seems to me that you know something about fighting the Old Ones yourselves. I have seen the warding runes on your gates, intended to keep Graghur out. I have been told that he is your enemy, as he is mine. His people attack you. He unleashes monsters in the corridors of the City in the Deeps. He plots to destroy you and make this whole city his. Is that not also the truth?"

Silence crashed down on the gathering. Kormak knew that he had touched a nerve. "Is that not the truth?" he asked, this time so quietly that the dwarves had to strain to hear.

"It is truth," said Ferik.

"It is truth," said Branhilde.

"It is truth," said Guttri.

"Then I believe I may be able to help you."

"And how would you do that?" asked Utti. There was a hushed note even in his hate-choked voice.

"I will kill Graghur for you." A tremendous uproar erupted. Kormak realised that he had most likely said the wrong thing. The dwarves surged forward, seemingly intent on tearing him apart with their bare hands.

"Get them out of here," Ferik bellowed to their escort.

# CHAPTER TWENTY-ONE

"WELL, AT LEAST we're still alive," said Boreas. Kormak stared at him. The cells walls pressed in oppressively.

"What did you say when you were up there," Sasha asked. "I thought they were going to tear you limb from limb. If those guards had not protected us, we would all be dead by now.

"The Guardian offered to destroy one of the beings they worship," said Karnea. She looked as if she did not quite know what to think of that, as if she was torn between admiration for his bravery and contempt for his stupidity.

"They are at war," Kormak said. "That much was obvious. I offered to do what their leaders must want but which is beyond their abilities."

"They could just take your sword and do it themselves."

"Look around you," said Kormak. "Have you seen a single dwarf carrying a sword? They call them forbidden weapons. I strongly doubt any of them could wield one except as a club. They could not beat Graghur with it."

"But you could?" Sasha asked. She was not mocking. She seemed to want to believe that he could.

"Yes," said Kormak. The doorway ground upwards. Guttri, Ferik and Branhilde were there. They were alone but all three of them were armed.

"What did you say?" Guttri asked. "You seem to have disturbed your companions."

Kormak told him.

"Do you really believe that, man?" Guttri asked.

"Yes. I have killed Old Ones before."

"You have borne that blade for a long time."

"More than twenty years."

"You would be considered little more than a child among our people," said Guttri.

Ferik said, "I have seen him wield it. He would kill many of our seasoned warriors if they fought with him."

"That might be useful," said Guttri. He looked at them. "Come, walk with me. I think there are matters we should discuss. Let there be plain speaking between us."

He gestured towards the doorway. There were no guards there, only the dwarvish leaders. Kormak wondered what was going on. Had he guessed right? Were they willing to make a deal with him to kill Graghur?

There was only one way to find out.

\*\*\*

The old dwarf limped along the corridor. The walls were marked with softly glowing runes. Beneath them were little stands of earth in which herbs grew. Guttri turned and looked directly at Kormak. "We are dying and we're desperate," he said. "I cannot say it before the clan but it is the truth. Once this place held thousands of dwarves, hundreds of our younglings, now there are barely enough of us to hold the gates and no children have been born in fifty years. In another few centuries we will be gone, leaving only this dead city as our monument and our vows unfulfilled."

He smiled and ran his hand through his limp beard. "Some of us will be gone sooner than others, so I can risk saying these things. I am a smith and I have no living son to pass my secrets on to. So another tradition dies and I pass the secrets to my nearest kin because the clan must have weapons. More things will be lost if I die before I teach all I know. I do not know what my father did, and he did not know what his father did and my apprentice will not know all that I know. We lose so much. Once we built this city for the Old Ones. Now we can barely forge an axe-blade.

"And today you come among us and show us a weapon that is beyond our skills to make, and not just because it was forged with forbidden runes, and you tell us that we have kin living elsewhere. I say, even though those kin may be betrayers, it is good to know they live."

Ferik looked away as though embarrassed but Branhilde smiled.

"Your kindred do not know you are here," said Karnea. "How did this happen?"

Both Ferik and Branhilde shot Guttri a warning look. He made a disparaging gesture and said, "Our secrets do us no good once we are dead." He made a circling gesture with his hand. "The warchief and the runekeeper both think I have become garrulous in my senility. Perhaps it is true but I will answer your questions if you will answer mine. There will be truth between us."

"Very well," said Kormak.

"Where was that sword made?"

"In the Hall of the Dwarves beneath Mount Aethelas."

"Where is that?"

"Hundreds of miles south of here. Why are you still here among the ruins of Khazduroth when everyone thinks you are dead?"

"We kept the faith," said Guttri proudly. "When all fell into chaos and war we kept the faith."

"What does that mean?"

"It is easier to show you, which I will in time."

"It seems to me that I am answering your questions and you are not answering mine," said Kormak.

"Be assured that I will. And now I will try harder to answer your first question. We are here because this is our home. It has always been our home. We built this city for the Eldrim but it was really our place. Our masters came and they went. They had palaces on mountain peaks and beneath the waves and amid the snows. They came here to meet and play politics, to commission new devices. We lived here, beneath their notice save when they wanted something. We recorded their deeds and contracts. We built the engines they required. We maintained their homes. We were their first, best and best-loved servants. Or so we thought."

Karnea was watching wide-eyed. Kormak guessed she had never heard such plain speaking from a dwarf before.

"The Old Ones turned against you?" Karnea asked.

"They did, but they turned against each other first."

"What do you mean?"

"There were those among the Eldrim who sought power over the others. They came to the elders of the clans and had them forge, in secret, the first of those dreadful blades, the like of which you carry."

"They wanted weapons that could easily kill the other Old Ones?" Kormak asked. "I thought that was forbidden."

"I would wager that it is forbidden for one of your people to murder another and I would also wager it still happens."

"It is no wonder they wanted it done in secret. A group armed with such weapons would be able to dominate all the other Old Ones," said Karnea.

"Only until the others armed themselves similarly," said Kormak. "And the Old Ones have all the time in the world."

"The weapons were made and the weapons were used, and we were blamed for it," said Guttri. "Eldrim killed Eldrim and as they did so, a terrible secret was revealed. Those who wielded those first weapons were pacted with the Shadow. They slew indiscriminately, took revenge on their enemies, made war on each other. But, in the end, it went as you suspected..." he nodded to Kormak. "The weapons fell into the hands of their enemies. Deaths multiplied. The City in the Deeps was abandoned by most of the Eldrim. They came only seeking weapons and in secret and they made the most dire threats. We could not but do what they wanted. Some of our folk fell into evil ways. Some tried to remain neutral. Some refused to serve the Shadow but who can know whether they did or not? Evil does not always come wearing an evil face.

"The war raged for centuries. The realms of the Old Ones were in chaos. All were suspicious of each other. None knew who secretly followed the Shadow. Rumours reached us of dark and terrible things occurring across the world, but we remained in our city and did as we always had. We obeyed. And then it happened... we were betrayed by our masters. They cursed us with a terrible plague."

"Why?"

"Other servitor races were rebelling. They did not want the secret of the making of forbidden weapons to be unleashed in the world. To be given to their enemies."

"They cursed you?" Karnea said. "That is terrible."

"The Old Ones think in terms of millennia," said Kormak.

"They cursed us and we died," said Guttri. "During the plagues we died in the tens of thousands. Husbands died in their wives arms. Children died weeping for succour from the gods who had abandoned us.

"The Plague did not kill all of us though. It is the nature of such things that some survive and are immune and their children are immune. When that failed, another curse was laid upon us. This curse altered the Underlings who had been our servants as we were the servants of the Eldrim. They mutated, became fierce and cunning and disobedient. They bred quickly. They fell to the Shadow and became fearsome foes, haunting the city they had helped us carve from the bones of the earth. They became stunted, misshapen things."

"Goblins," Karnea said. She nodded her head.

"The followers of Graghur," said Guttri. "The ones you fought."

"They are the descendants of your servants," said Karnea. Her voice was hushed. Her hand had formed a grip on an imaginary pen.

"They have descended a long way from what they were. Once they were gentle creatures, passive, bred for labour and for obedience. The plagues changed them, almost as if that was the intent." The old dwarf looked at his hulking tattooed barbarous companions and then looked ironically at the statue of a noble civilised dwarf that occupied an alcove above him. "They changed us too. The few that survived. Some of our people found terrible rage in their hearts. Some swore to the Shadow and were saved and vanished. Some slid away, seeking sanctuary elsewhere, hoping to find a refuge. One clan of smiths broke into the forbidden armouries and took a cache of weapons. We thought them slain in the Long Dying but their mark is upon your blade. I am guessing they still seek revenge on our masters."

"I can understand why," said Kormak. "I cannot understand why you do not."

"Because not all of the Eldrim turned against us. Some sought to aid us, to preserve us. They warded us through the plague, saved those they could, fought the ones who would destroy us. They protected us and we kept the faith with them. It is what we were bred to do. We are sworn to serve and it is not in our nature to break our oaths."

"What became of the Old Ones who protected you?"

"They fought a long grinding war against those who would exterminate us. Eventually all save the most determined fell away on both sides, leaving behind only a few committed utterly to the conflict. The war tore the City in the Deeps apart. They warred with dreadful sorceries so potent that even if they did not destroy outright, their targets were crippled for centuries or longer. The plagues they unleashed began to change even the Eldrim, crippling them, twisting them, driving them mad. In the end only two were left to fight, the rest grew weary. One of those was Graghur. The other was... well, see for yourself!"

They had entered a great chamber. A dozen gigantic statues of Old Ones stood around the walls. In the centre was a great stone sarcophagus with a crystalline lid. The dwarves all knelt and made a complex symbol over their hearts before they advanced up the stairs to it. Kormak knelt and from force of habit made the Elder Sign of the Sun then he rose to approach the coffin in which the Old One lay. The others did the same.

Looking down, Kormak saw the face of a dead goddess. She resembled the dwarves in some ways but her features were finer. She was beautiful and strange, with her long hair like filaments of spun glass and eyes black as the pits of night. She was garbed in a robe of fishscale silver with runes of iron on her shoulders. A staff marked with symbols of power was across her chest. On her brow was a circlet bearing the sign of the first-born children of the Moon. A great wound marked her chest, a single drop of blood emerged from it, redder than any human blood would have been.

"Behold Morloqua," said Guttri. "The Mother of Dwarves, our creator. She did not abandon her children. And we will not abandon her. She lies sleeping until she can heal from her wounds. We watch over her still."

He made a complex sign over the sleeping goddess with his right hand and then led them from the chamber. They walked in silence through the empty halls.

# CHAPTER TWENTY-TWO

THEY SAT IN Guttri's chambers, on benches that had clearly been made for the comfort of dwarves, not humans. A bed of stone inscribed with runes stood in one corner. At its foot was a chest. There were no other furnishings.

"What happened to the Mother?" Karnea asked. Her voice was very quiet and there had been a note of almost religious awe in it since she had seen the Old One.

"She was wounded by Graghur. She withdrew to her stasis coffin to attempt to purify herself and there she has remained. Graghur's sorcery is strong though and she has not been able to heal herself of the poisonous effects."

"Why has Graghur returned to seek vengeance now?" Karnea asked.

"We do not know," said Guttri. "He and the Mother fought their final battle millennia ago. He was terribly wounded and fled before her. She drove him out of the city and ordered the gates sealed with runes of warding and concealment so that we would not be found again by our enemies. She was so badly depleted herself that she collapsed thereafter and was placed within her sarcophagus. The process has taken longer than any of us ever expected but still we keep the faith. Graghur abandoned his spawn in the depths and we have warred with them since." Kormak struggled to understand what the dwarf was saying. The word depleted clearly had some significance he could not quite comprehend.

"When did Graghur return?" Sasha asked, after what had been said was explained to her.

"About sixty moons ago," said Guttri. Karnea translated.

"That would have been about the time the Elder Signs on the gates were smashed," Sasha said. "He would have been able to get back in then."

Guttri said, "New interlopers entered the city before Graghur returned. They were men, other fallen servants of the Eldrim, and we assumed they were of the Shadow. We avoided them but we could not avoid Graghur. He came himself wearing the shape he had of old, resembling a mighty dwarf. We held parlay with him in the great plaza beyond our gates. He spoke fair words and said he had repented and begged to see the Mother again. We refused them, though some like Utti thought it blasphemy."

"We would not open the gates for him and he departed into the depths and shortly thereafter goblins and other evil things started to multiply. Great monsters were unleashed in the Underhalls."

"Graghur created the monsters," said Kormak.

Guttri twisted his head in the dwarf equivalent of a nod. "He is a fleshmoulder. He is the father of the Underlings just as Morloqua is the Mother of Dwarves. He hates her and he hates those who are her children."

"And if we slay Graghur for you, you will help us?"

"What is it you seek?"

Karnea told him of the runes and the netherium. The old dwarf made a chopping gesture with his broad-fingered hand that indicated a negative.

"You will not help us?" Karnea said. Her voice was plaintive, her eyes downcast.

Guttri again made the chopping gesture. "I would if I could but I have not the skill to make the runes of which you speak. You must talk with Branhilde the Beautiful about such things. It would be her choice whether to share her secrets. If she has knowledge of the things you call Lost Runes. It may be your people know more of such things than we do now. As I said before we have lost much."

"What about the netherium?" Kormak asked.

Guttri's smile held grim amusement. "That is a bargain I cannot make in good faith."

"What do you mean?" Karnea said.

"You will never get the netherium unless you kill Graghur."

"Why?" Kormak asked.

"Because he controls the mine from which it comes. It is all in Underling territory now."

*** 

A soft scratching came on the door. Guttri raised his head. His beard twitched faintly. His nostrils dilated. A frown creased his features.

"I smell death," he said. The door opened and Verlek tumbled through it. A trail of blood stained the corridor behind his back. The red fluid pumped from his chest. Agony wracked his features. He was quite plainly dying.

"Treachery," he groaned and collapsed at Guttri's feet. The old dwarf bent over him and touched his brow.

"What happened?"

"Utti! Utti!" Verlek said. "He came to me after the moot—told me he was wrong. He had been sent to bring Kormak's blade to him. He took it and then he stabbed me with it... I am dying."

"Utti has my sword?" Kormak said. A cold hand gripped his heart.

"Aye," said Verlek. "I am sorry, Kormak. He took me off guard. I betrayed your trust and I have not repaid my blood-debt."

He reached upwards in a gesture of farewell then his muscular tattooed arm slumped to the ground. All life had spilled out of him.

Guttri rose to his feet and bellowed. "Find Utti! Have him brought to me. I would have an explanation of this!"

Kormak paused for a last look at the sad, lost face of Verlek before he followed Guttri down the ramp towards the vault into the Dwarfhold. They made for the Wall of Skulls.

\*\*\*

A score of dwarves surrounded them. All of them were armed and all of them were wary and more than a few of them threw suspicious looks at Kormak and his companions. The central flame flickered and shadows danced across the rows and rows of skulls.

Ferik stomped in. A look of controlled anger burned in his face. The tendrils of his beard writhed with fury. "Utti is no longer within the Dwarfhold," he said. "He left by the southern postern gate. I have sent Mankri to track him. "

He tossed a sack at Kormak's feet. "He has taken your sword with him. As far as I can tell all the rest of your possessions are there."

Kormak opened the sack and found his Elder Signs and the other equipment Karnea had brought with her. She took the rune torque up and put it on her arm.

"Why has he taken the blade?" Karnea asked. "What good would it do him?"

"Perhaps he has gone to attempt to slay Graghur himself." Ferik said. His tone was doubtful.

Guttri shook his head. "Utti is not the sort to seek glory. Nor is he the bravest of dwarves."

"Then why?" Ferik demanded harshly. "And why slay my only surviving son."

"You know why," Guttri said.

Ferik turned and looked away. He squeezed his eyes shut. The muscles in his neck tightened. His fingers went white around the grips of his weapon. "No."

"He always desired Branhilde. He took it badly when she chose you. And he always hated the boy. You know that."

"No dwarf would do this though..."

"Verlek is dead. The sword is gone and Utti with it." Guttri let the words hang in the air.

Ferik let out a howl of terrible rage and grief. "I will rip his head off with my bare hands," he said. "No forbidden weapon will save him."

"The question remains why he took it," Guttri said.

"My son is dead and all you do is ask foolish questions," Ferik said. Guttri's response was mild.

"The question is not foolish. The survival of our people rests on the answer. Without the blade we cannot slay Graghur. Utti knows that."

"Utti is a dwarf. He would not see us all dead."

"Not us all. You are correct."

Ferik tilted his head to one side. "You think he intends to bargain with Graghur. Graghur will laugh at him and order his spawn to take the blade."

"Perhaps. There are oaths that are binding on the Eldrim as they are on us." He looked at Kormak who nodded to confirm this. "If he was to hide the blade somewhere..."

"Graghur might torture the whereabouts of the blade out of him," Karnea said.

Ferik laughed. "Stubborn as stone are dwarves. Pain does but make us more so."

Guttri said, "With this blade Graghur can set himself up to lord it over other Old Ones. And Utti can show him all the secret ways into our hold. Or open the runegates for him and his people."

"I hope you are wrong," said Ferik.

"So do I, but I fear I am not."

"What now?"

"We wait for Mankri to return. He may overtake Utti and at very least he'll be able to tell us where he has gone."

*\*\**

"Utti entered Graghur's mine," said Mankri. He was relatively slender for a dwarf, his build of almost human proportions. His face was narrow and his expression grim. His beard did not seem to writhe quite as much as the other dwarfs'. "He went in there and he took the blade with him."

"So much for him stowing it somewhere," said Ferik. "One way or another I think we can assume that Graghur has the blade now."

"There was no smell of blood or a struggle," said Mankri. "I would have expected the goblins to shred him and take his gear. I would have smelled the scent of that."

"It's almost as if he was welcomed," said Mankri.

"Utti talked with Graghur's emissaries when they came, he talked with Graghur himself many times," Guttri said. "It is possible he was recognised."

"Or maybe he has been there before. Utti wandered alone through the Underhalls many times," said Ferik.

"So have may others," said Guttri. "Yourself not excepted."

"It does not matter how or why," said Kormak. "The fact is that Graghur now has my blade. A dwarf-forged runeblade is in the hands of an Old One."

"Why would he want to wield it?" said Mankri. "One nick with the death rune might be fatal to him."

"He does not need to use it as a weapon," said Guttri. "He just needs it to stab..."

He could not finish the sentence, nor did he need to. Mankri's nostrils flared and his eyes went wide. "He could kill the Mother of Dwarves with it."

"We need to make sure that does not happen," said Ferik.

"Yes," said Guttri. "The question is how."

"We must call another Dwarfmoot and let the clan know what is happening," said Ferik. "Go summon the folk!"

Mankri went.

*\*\**

The eyes of the Dwarfmoot were all focused on Kormak with a mixture of resentment and hatred after Guttri explained why they had been summoned. The dwarves all seemed to blame him for bringing the sword among them. Their stares were unnerving for he knew dwarves had a talent for holding a grudge.

"Utti has taken the accursed weapon," Guttri said. "And I fear that Graghur will return bearing it and the secrets of our hold."

"What are we to do?" someone called from the crowd. "Graghur cannot be defeated without the blade."

Kormak raised his hand and Ferik gestured for him to mount the step. "There is only one thing to be done. We must reclaim the sword"

"It may already be in Graghur's clutches," said Branhilde. Her face was lined with grief but her voice was cold as winter frost.

"Then we just need to wait and he will show up at our gates with his army," said Ferik. His smile showed he was making a bleak jest but his words were in all essentials true.

"There is another way," said Guttri. Ferik's bleak expression told Kormak that he already knew what the ancient dwarf was going to suggest and did not like it. "We could take the war to him."

"You are not suggesting we march into his lair and demand that he hand the traitor back to us along with the stolen weapon, are you?" Ferik's could not keep the sardonic tone from his voice.

"It might be better than waiting here for him to come and slay us and the one we protect."

Ferik smiled. "It would make a heroic tale, for sure, but there would be none left to tell it."

"If we can sneak into his camp we may be able to recover the blade," said Guttri. "With it we can kill him."

"It is suicide," said Ferik. "We would all die."

"Not all of us," said Guttri. "This is the sort of task best suited to a small group. A warband might not be able to infiltrate the mine but a small party might."

Ferik considered his words. "How many?"

"You are the warleader, you decide."

Kormak realised that he was going to have to reclaim his blade. Without it there was no chance of getting out of this place anyway. It was simply a case of waiting for doom to overtake them.

"I will go," said Kormak. "It is my blade and I am the one with the best chance of slaying Graghur."

"That I will take as true," said Ferik. "I am going for I would have words with Utti. I will take Mankri. He knows his way around the mines. I will take half a dozen volunteers. Any more risks leaving the gates unguarded at a time when they must be held."

"I will go," said Karnea. "I don't want to but I don't want to be left behind either."

Boreas and Sasha looked at them, and Karnea explained what was being said. "You three should remain here where it's safe," Kormak said. He was thinking of his orders from the Grand Master and his promise to Tam.

"I'm not being left here on my own," said Sasha. "These dwarves look as if they are just waiting to cut my throat."

"You might need a healer," said Karnea. "And my wards and the rune may help. If you don't get the blade, it will only a matter of time before Graghur comes to the Dwarfhold and slays us all. We have a better chance together."

"In that case, I'm going too," said Boreas. "I am your bodyguard."

"Before we go I need to feed the Mankh rune flames," Karnea said.

Ferik nodded his agreement. "It will be so. Such power may prove useful to us."

"I need some more runestones for my stonethrower," said Sasha. "If the dwarves could provide some I would be grateful..."

Karnea translated. Ferik barked orders. Dwarves scuttled off to find what was needed.

Kormak looked out at the crowd. The dwarves clamoured for his attention. He picked them out one by one. Despair gnawed at his heart. He had lost his blade and without it he had no chance of killing Graghur, much less of keeping the others alive.

# CHAPTER TWENTY-THREE

GUTTRI AND THE remaining dwarves waved them good-bye from the gates of the Dwarfhold. Ferik embraced Branhilde, his beard intertwining with her hair in a gesture that seemed curiously intimate. Once they parted Ferik turned and did not look back. Neither did Kormak. There was no reason for him to do so. It was just one more place that he was leaving behind him as he had left countless others.

He could tell the others did not quite feel the same way. They had gotten used to being inside the Dwarfhold. If it had not been safe, it had at least felt predictable, which was the next best thing as far as most people were concerned. He had learned long ago that no place was truly safe.

Karnea glanced back nervously and polished her glasses. Sasha glanced out into the darkness fearfully. The dwarves had provided her with a pouch full of runestones for her weapon. Boreas hefted his new warhammer and tried a practise swing.

"Better than my last," he said. "Better balanced. Better made."

"I'm glad it makes you happy," said Kormak.

Boreas gave him a mock frown. "I never said I was happy."

Kormak lifted the axe the dwarves had loaned him. It felt strange in his hand, after all these years of wielding a sword. Of course, he knew how to use it. He had been trained with all the weapons he was ever likely to be called on to wield back when he was a novice. It irritated him that he was not entirely comfortable with the weapon now. His life might depend on it.

They marched back across the bridge. There were no signs of Graghur's army. According to Mankri, it had retreated all the way back to the mines. Ferik sent him scouting ahead anyway. The dwarf chieftain kept them moving at a tremendous pace through the darkened corridors. Everglow lanterns probed the darkness just ahead of them, but Kormak knew enough about the dwarves now to know they were not relying on their eyes. Their ears, their noses and even their beards all relayed them information as they sensed vibrations through the floor. They had many more ways than a man to know what was happening around them in the long darkness. They were very far from blind. The lights were more for the benefit of the humans than the dwarves.

They took a ramp that spiralled downwards. Kormak wondered how far below the ground the City in the Deeps went. Sometimes it felt like they were burrowing towards the heart of the world. Perhaps if they kept going long enough they would emerge in the Kingdoms of Dust.

The ceilings began to lower and were more crude-looking. Kormak walked up beside Ferik. "Was this the earliest built part of the city?" he asked.

"No, our ancestors dug down from the original mines and caverns. This was merely the part most of the Eldrim never came to. It was the home of the Underlings long ago. There were more workshops down here and those industries the Eldrim did not like to look on. The smell of some of them lingers on even after all these years.

"I cannot smell anything."

"You do not have the nose of a dwarf."

"It would look out of place on my face," Kormak said. Ferik gave a short barking sound that it took Kormak a moment to realise was a laugh. He repeated the words to the other dwarves, and they too made the noise.

"Only the poorest of our ancestors would have dwelled here. Those with no reason to visit the courts of the Eldrim. The rememberers and the lawsmiths and runesculptors all lived above near the palaces. Some of them dwelled in homes almost as splendid as the least of the Eldrim. At least so the old stories say."

The dwarf seemed happy to talk. Most likely it took his mind off other things. "Are your cities so splendid?"

"We have nothing like this on the surface."

"Likely this must all seem very strange to you then."

"Aye," Kormak said. "It does."

"Why did you really agree to come with us?" The question came out of nowhere. Kormak wondered if this bluntness was simply a dwarvish trait or whether it was meant to shock him into an unguarded response.

"I want my sword back."

"As simple as that?"

"I swore an oath a long time ago, to protect my people from the Old Ones. I cannot fulfil that oath without that blade and I would be shamed to go back to my order having lost it."

"It seems that your people and mine may not be so different then. You know what it means to keep an oath."

"I confess I feel the need to repay Utti for taking it."

Ferik shot him an angry glance. "Utti is mine, Guardian of the Dawn. He owes me blood for the life of my son. I will take his skull for that although it goes against all our laws."

Kormak shrugged. If Utti got in his way, he would kill him. Otherwise Ferik was welcome to his vengeance. They strode along in silence after that, through low ceilinged halls that sometimes gave way to vast open chambers full of pillars. Kormak felt a draft of hot air blowing then and wondered where it came from. He guessed that given time he could trace it to its source but time was a thing that was in short supply now.

"How long till we reach the mines?" he asked Ferik.

"Ten thousand strides or more," the dwarf replied. "Do not worry we will get there soon enough."

Kormak fell back to walk with his fellows.

"It feels like we've been down here for months," said Karnea.

"It always feels that way once you get past the first few hours," said Sasha. "You lose all sense of time. After a while it seems like you've always been down here and the sun is just a memory of a dream."

"I hope not," said Karnea. "I would like to look on it again before I die."

Kormak heard the fear in her voice. Karnea believed she was already as good as dead. She had no hope of ever seeing the surface again. Yet that did not keep her from looking around and drinking in the sights. It was something Kormak understood. He never felt so alive and alert as when he was on the brink of death.

"At least we are out of that cell," said Boreas. "I never liked those."

"You've spent time in the cells?" Sasha asked. Her tone was teasing.

"What mercenary has not?" Boreas replied. "You hit town with a purse full of silver and you spend it on booze and song and women till it's gone. Mishaps occur and the local law-makers are rarely amused or forgiving. What about you, Guardian, have you ever spent time in a cell?"

"More than I care to remember," said Kormak. "I liked it no more than you."

They walked on, talking of inconsequential things, deliberately not speaking about what was really on their minds.

\*\*\*

The corridors had taken on a rough look and Kormak could see that iron rails had been set in the floor. He assumed they had been put there for ore-carts. Ahead of them was a large area where dozens of such tracks met. There were metal wheeled-carts there and signs that goblins had passed this way. The air smelled of goblin piss and wolf excrement. Somewhere overhead Kormak thought he heard great batwings flutter.

"The mines go a long way down from here," said Ferik.

"Guards?" Kormak asked.

"Not yet. There are too many shafts and galleries and not even the goblins have sufficient numbers to watch them all. We killed a great many of them. Graghur must regret ordering an assault on our hold."

"But you've still sent Mankri ahead to make sure."

"There is no sense in taking undue risks," said Ferik. "And he is a very stealthy dwarf."

They pushed on into the mines. These did not look much like any mine Kormak had ever been in. The floors were paved and the walls and ceilings were as regular as those of the city up above. If it had not been for the metal rails in the floor and the absence of building fronts,

Kormak would not have known they were in a mine at all.

They pushed on down. Galleries, long worked-out, ran away from the corridors. They were much lower than the ceilings in the Underhalls. They looked as if they were intended for the use of people the height of dwarves. Goblins would have no problem living here but Kormak felt the urge to constantly duck his head.

He could hear strange sounds in the distance now; clattering, banging, high-pitched screaming and once, an odd roaring noise that reminded him of Yellow Eye and the Slitherer.

Ferik saw him pause and said, "Yes, this is where Graghur breeds his monsters. They say he keeps the tame ones and drives the most savage and rebellious out into the corridors of the city."

"So we can look forward to meeting more like the Slitherer," said Kormak.

"Are you worried about meeting one without your sword?" Ferik asked.

"I would be worried about meeting one even with it."

"Then you seem more sensible than my son made you sound, may the Ancestors welcome his soul." There was a weight of sadness and anger in the dwarf's voice when he talked about Verlek.

Mankri appeared in front of them, emerging from a side corridor.

"It is as it always was," he said. "They do not watch the shafts in the eightieth gallery. We can enter the Deeps there."

"You have been this way before?" Kormak asked.

Mankri nodded. "I once went all the way to the Chamber of Monsters just to see if I could."

"How do you avoid being spotted?" Mankri tapped one of the runes on his arm. Kormak had not seen its like before.

"That confuses the goblins noses and I am very quiet when I want to be. Patient, too."

"You have done well," said Ferik. "If we can use the shafts we will reach the heart of the goblins realm."

"Unless Graghur and his court have moved," said Mankri.

"Perhaps it would be best to look at the bright side," said Ferik.

"For me, that is the bright side." Mankri gave them a cheery grin. It seemed the worse things looked, the more cheerful he became.

***

Ahead of them lay a long, steeply sloping shaft, even more constricted than the previous ones. Moving on all fours the dwarves had a lot less problems negotiating it than Kormak and his fellow humans. He had to crawl and twist and scuttle. The hilt of the axe he had hung over his shoulder ground along against the ceiling, slowing him down and making a grinding noise until he managed to adjust its position. Eventually he had to turn and clamber down as the shaft went near vertical.

His hands scraped against rough stone and his shoulders began to ache from the strain. His palms were slippery with sweat. The walls pressed in all around him. His breathing became forced. He wondered what would happen if he let go. He imagined slithering down a very long, steep slope, banging against the walls as he went until eventually he smashed to a halt a long way below.

He kept climbing down. He told himself that the dwarves had been this way before and must know what they were doing. A small niggling part of his mind pointed out that they had never done this with humans before and it was quite possible they had made a miscalculation.

Finally his feet touched flat ground and he realised that he was on the level again. It was dark and his sense of being enclosed did not let up. All the weight of the mountains seemed to be pressing down on him.

A powerful hand landed on his shoulder, and he felt the faint, tickling touch of a dwarf's beard as it rippled over him in the dark. The image of a cockroach's feelers flickered through his mind and he fought it down.

"Stand clear," said Ferik's voice, out of the utter blackness. "The others are coming down."

Kormak let himself be pulled out of the way. He heard something scraping above him and then a muted curse. Sasha was down. "Kormak, are you there?" Her voice sounded almost panicked.

"Yes," he said as calmly as he could. Displaced air warned him and then a hand quested out of the darkness and touched his face.

"It doesn't have a beard so I am guessing it's you," she said. Her giggle was on the verge of hysteria.

Boreas and Karnea emerged. Shortly thereafter something bumped down the shaft. Boreas muttered thanks and he realised that the dwarves must have lowered his hammer on a rope and then given it to him. He wished they had thought about that before his axe had almost gotten him stuck in the shaft. It was too late to bring it up now. He would remember such a thing in the future, if he had one.

Once again the everglow lantern was revealed and Kormak saw that he was standing in a low rough-hewn corridor. He could see water gurgling away near his feet. It was brownish and foul-smelling and he wondered where it came from and where it was going to.

Ferik said, "We must go slowly and quietly now. We are coming to the heart of Graghur's realm."

# CHAPTER TWENTY-FOUR

THEY FOLLOWED THE evil-smelling stream along the tunnel. With every step the foul stench grew increasingly strong, a stomach-churning mix of sour milk, sulphur and strange alchemicals. Karnea raised her hand to her mouth. Sasha covered the lower part of her face with a scarf. Boreas contented himself with wrinkling his nose and narrowing his eyes.

Kormak's heart beat faster. They were within the core of their enemy's realm now. He had no idea where his blade was to be found. He was going to have to trust to the dwarves' senses and his own wits. It seemed only logical that either Utti or Graghur would now have the blade. Of course, they were both likely to be surrounded by goblin guards.

And if that were not bad enough, the Old One would be invincible if Kormak could not get his hands on his blade. He told himself that was not true—Graghur could still be hurt by normal weapons, possibly even temporarily stopped if his head were chopped off or a dagger driven into his heart. He just could not be killed. He would just have to do what he could, with the weapons that he had. If the Old One had his blade and could be overcome even temporarily,

Kormak could finish the fight.

"Why are you grinning, Guardian?" Karnea asked him.

"I was thinking about Graghur."

"I hope you never think about me that way. You look like a man contemplating murder."

"I am contemplating killing."

"You enjoy it, don't you?" Karnea said. Kormak considered her words. He wanted Graghur dead and he wanted his blade back. Would he take pleasure in slaying Graghur? If he was honest with himself, the answer was yes. "I do," he said.

"You are a born killer."

Kormak shook his head. "No more than any other man. I was trained to it and I am good at it. Over the years I have acquired a taste for it. You would too if you lived my life."

"I doubt it," she said. She sounded quite certain of that.

They emerged into a vast chamber and it became obvious what the source of the smell was. Huge pits had been dug from the ground, and they were filled to overflowing with the brownish fluid. Looking into the nearest, Kormak could see a massive shape writhing and twitching as though in troubled sleep. It resembled a goblin grown to four times its normal size with a lower body something like that of a horse.

"This is where Graghur breeds his hybrids," Karnea said.

"This is where the Slitherer and Yellow Eye and those other monsters were birthed. Some of these creatures will be soldiers in Graghur's army. Others will be unleashed into the Underhalls," said Ferik.

Boreas looked at the monster and said, "Ugly beast. This Graghur must be a dark and terrible wizard."

"He is a Shaper," said Karnea. "Many of the Old Ones were. They could bend the stuff of life to their will, father new races, create monsters, change living things into new forms."

Ferik asked her to translate and then nodded. "They say that, in ancient times, he and the Mother were rivals in the art. This was one of the reasons for the bitterness of their hatred. Some say they were lovers and that their love turned sour."

"I do not think the Old Ones know love as we do," said Kormak.

"They certainly understand hatred," said Ferik.

"I am not sure they feel any emotions we would understand," said Kormak.

"The same could be said of man and dwarf."

"There are words for love and hate and fear in both our languages," said Karnea.

"The Eldrim have those words too."

"Can we be sure they mean the same things to each of us? Your eyes are different from ours. You may have no words for certain colours we can see. How can I be certain those words describe the same thing?"

"This is all very fascinating," said Kormak, "but it takes us no closer to reclaiming my blade."

The dwarf and the sorceress looked at each other and then at him. The dwarf shrugged. Karnea smiled.

They passed cables of living flesh that ran from huge bladders of some leathery material. When Kormak looked closely he could see that the bladders had vestigial eyes and were living creatures themselves, some form of grossly mutated goblin. Clutching the walls were other goblin-like creatures, with massive bloated stomachs and breasts. They looked like certain ants he had seen in a broken hill, whose bodies had been turned into great receptacles to hold food for their kindred.

As had happened so often in the past, when he was confronted by the work of the Old Ones, he felt an oppressive sense of the vast, alien strangeness of their knowledge. They had forgotten more than men had learned in all their history, and they had bent that knowledge to many awful purposes.

Graghur looked like the meanest of monsters but it was a shape he had chosen for himself when he could look like anything he wanted. Here was proof of the depth of his knowledge and the power of his magic. He had created these pits in which monsters were being born and Kormak had no idea why. He might have been creating an army or simply probing the secrets of life, the way some alchemists did. When Graghur died all this knowledge would be removed from the world. So much had been lost already and Kormak had been responsible for some of the destruction. If he lived he would be responsible for more.

Even if he won, he would not change the fact that compared to Graghur he was an insect. To the Old Ones, he was like one of those biting flies that spread the plague. He felt very small. That was one of the reasons he enjoyed slaying the Eldrim.

Somehow he did not feel like telling Karnea that.

***

They made their way across the huge chamber, moving slowly, treading quietly. Kormak saw the distant shadowy figures of several great goblins hauling barrels to the pools and dumping their contents into the murky fluid.

He wished they had half a dozen good bowmen. He could have killed all the goblins swiftly, but ranged weapons were not something dwarves were good with. They seemed to rely on war engines and explosives. Explosives they had but those would only give away their position to the sharp-eared goblins.

They passed another pit. This one held a less well-developed inhabitant. It did not have any skin as yet, merely muscle and vein. It looked as if it had been flayed alive. It did not move. Perhaps it was dead or dormant. They moved beyond one of the huge bladder creatures. Its stomach expanded and distended. Something pulsed through the flesh cable leading from it to the nearest pool.

Ferik wrinkled his nose. His beard twitched, tendrils writhing. "I smell Utti," he said.

Kormak looked at him astonished. The dwarf must have a nose like a bloodhound. "How can you smell anything over this stink?"

"How can you not?"

"You can lead us to him?"

"Yes. Given time."

"And the fact we will have to find our way through an army of goblins."

Ferik let his beard touch the floor. "There are several hundred. They took a lot of casualties at the gates of the Dwarfhold. Graghur has not had time to breed more."

"That's all right then. The ten of us should be more than enough to see off a mere few hundred," Kormak said.

"I like your attitude, man," Ferik said. Kormak wondered whether the dwarves had any word for irony in their language. "But we will need to be cunning and strike by stealth. I catch a whiff of the Eldrim now. He is ahead of us, I am guessing in the great central chamber. It is the heart of the mine. I used to play there when I was a lad."

They passed another pit. In this one was a monstrous goblin centaur, a hybrid of Yellow Eye and a great dire wolf. It looked awake.

Its eyes glared back at him ferociously and it began to reach out. A huge hand emerged from the fluid. Kormak stepped back, readying his axe.

The monster dragged itself up and out and gave a great gurgling cough, spraying fluid through the air, splattering everything nearby. It snarled revealing shark-like teeth and reached for him with long sharp claws.

"So much for being stealthy," Ferik said. He lashed out at the monster with his axe. Boreas leapt forward, hitting it with his hammer and over-balancing it back into the pit. Kormak could see some of the great goblins looking around, attracted by the noise.

Sasha cursed, raised her stonethrower and fired a runestone at them. The explosion hurled the goblins through the air, garments alight, flesh torn. One of them tumbled into a pool. The fluid bubbled and another massive figure erupted from it, something that looked like a monstrous goblin body with the head of an octopus. It grabbed a goblin and dragged the screaming creature towards its maw.

"Let's get out of here," said Ferik. They raced through the archway and found themselves in a huge central chamber. It was at the bottom of an enormous pit, with makeshift elevators, running up and down the sides. Around the edges were scores of archways just like the one they had come through. Kormak guessed they represented other galleries running off into the depths. Metal railings for carts, and enormous slag piles rearing beside them reinforced that conclusion.

In the centre of the chamber, on a monstrous throne, lolled the gigantic form of Graghur. In front of him, dressed in a motley, with a ball and chain on his leg was Utti. As they entered Graghur looked up and smiled.

"What is this?" he asked in a booming voice that echoed through the caverns. "Visitors? And we have not prepared a feast to welcome them! Well, no matter, they shall provide the feast themselves."

He laughed and then threw back his head and howled. Hundreds of chittering, squeaking calls answered him. From a dozen of the entrances goblins poured. Half a dozen wolves, including the giant one that Graghur had used as a steed erupted as if from a pit at his feet. More goblin voices sounded from above them.

If they waited, they would simply be overwhelmed. There was nothing to do but attack now. Kormak raised the axe and charged. The others were right behind him.

A few missiles arced down from galleries above them. The goblins had not yet had time to realise that only a few intruders were attacking them. Darts clattered to the ground near Kormak but most of them fell behind him.

Laughing Graghur bounded towards him, brandishing a weapon in each of his four hands. Kormak recognised one of them as his own blade. He was surprised the Old One had the nerve to carry it. The wolves and their giant pack leader were right behind Graghur. Squads of goblins raced to join the fray.

Kormak and Graghur crossed blades. The Old One was fast and incredibly strong and Kormak was far less used to wielding an axe than a sword. It was all he could do to parry Graghur's blows.

Boreas leapt into the fray, dwarf maul smashing down, taking advantage of the Old One's concentration on Kormak. The force of the blow sent Graghur reeling back. The links on his chainmail coat were broken.

Graghur laughed madly as if the pain only amused him. Perhaps it did. Kormak had met Old Ones who chose to feel pain as pleasure and pleasure as pain. Graghur bounced back, slashing at Boreas with his scimitar. Boreas parried it, but a blow from Kormak's own runeblade cut through the big man's armour and sliced his flesh. Blood poured from the open wound and Boreas fell to the ground.

A howling pack of wolves raced forward. Flame belched from the nostrils of their leader. One of Sasha's runestones impacted in the middle of them. The lesser wolves howled as the blast bowled them over and set light to their fur. The leader kept on coming, immune to the effect of the fire blast.

Utti raised the ball and chain attached to his ankle. He started to swing it as a weapon. Kormak could not decide whether he was intending to attack the interlopers or Graghur with it. Maybe the dwarf could not decide himself. Ferik made up his mind for him, charging at Utti, yelling, "Die traitor!"

Utti whirled the massive metal ball around, but Ferik was too fast for him, pouncing like a springing tiger, rolling under the spinning ball and smashing his axe into Utti's leg. Utti overbalanced, pulled down by the weight of his own improvised weapon. Overcome with rage, Ferik dropped his axe and wrapped his hands around Utti's throat. He began to twist.

Kormak leapt forward striking at Graghur again. The Old One parried effortlessly with one of his scimitars. Kormak struck again and this time the Old One did as he had hoped and parried with Kormak's own sword. Kormak hooked it with the blade of his axe and twisted, wrenching it free from Graghur's grip and sending it flying off through the air. He barely had time to leap back before the Old One's counter-attack almost beheaded him.

"I see your plan, human," said Graghur. "You seek to take back the gift my friend Utti brought me and use it against me. Very clever but it will not work."

The Old One attacked like a four armed whirlwind. A storm of blades blew around Kormak. He ducked and weaved and parried desperately and still he bled from a dozen cuts. His arms, legs and sides burned and he was not sure whether he had taken a major wound or not. Sometimes it took seconds, even minutes to feel the full pain of such.

He could not find any space to launch a counter-attack, and even if he had been able to, it would not have mattered. Graghur was berserk and he did not fear the axe Kormak carried. He could take a wound from it and know he would not die. His own blades would chop Kormak to pieces.

Out of the corner of his eyes Kormak saw goblins pouring down the walls from the caves above. The great wolf bounded passed him to seek out Sasha. Mankri and the others were surrounded by a horde of foes. As the wolf breathed fire, Karnea stepped into the flames. She did not burn. The flame formed a halo around her and then vanished as if breathed in by a dragon. The runic armlet burned brightly on her arm, glowing more intensely as it absorbed more energy.

Karnea spoke the name of the rune. A symbol of flame, exactly the same as the one on her arm, appeared between her outstretched hands. The sorceress spoke the name again and its glow intensified. More and more fire was being drawn from the wolf. It shrivelled and shrank until it was utterly gone, all of its blazing life force absorbed. Then Karnea spoke the name of the rune for a third time. The luminous symbol hovering before her flickered through the air towards Graghur.

Kormak had barely enough time to look away and doing so almost got him killed. He only managed to get his axe clumsily in the way of one of Graghur's scimitars. The force of the stroke cut through the haft and sent the blade *thunking* down into Kormak's chest. The impact knocked him off his feet and below the strike of Graghur's other attacks. The pain was shocking and Kormak wondered what was broken.

He rolled away just as the flame-rune exploded. Tentacles of fire lashed out at Graghur and his followers. The flash was visible even through his closed eyelids. Goblins screamed. Dwarves cursed. Graghur wailed as if burned. Kormak rolled, side still aching, to where his sword had fallen. He reached out and his fingers closed on its familiar hilt. A savage snarl twisted his lips. New strength flooded into him as he rose to his feet.

He raced forward towards Graghur once again. The Old One's skin was blackened. Smoke rose from his hide. His eyes emitted huge green tears. He cast one of his scimitars. It turned end over end and buried itself in Karnea's chest. She fell to the ground, eyes wide open, blood dribbling from her lips. Graghur turned to face Kormak now. His eyes widened in horror when he saw what Kormak held in his hands. He took a step backward even as Kormak ran at him.

Kormak's attacks had far greater speed and fluidity than they had when he was wielding an axe, and the Old One flinched away from them, knowing what would happen if the blade bit into his flesh. He wielded both his scimitars with great speed and skill but now he fought defensively, calling out for help in the chittering language of the goblins.

A wave of the small creatures threw themselves forward, interposing themselves between the Guardian and their king. Kormak chopped them down and kept going, determined to put an end to Graghur if it was the last thing he did. He forced thoughts of Karnea from his mind. There was no time no to try and treat her wounds. She might already be dead. He could not afford for his concentration to slip while he battled the Old One.

Kormak and Graghur fought their way to the edge of the cavern, to where one of the elevators stood. It was operated manually by turning a wheel connected to a system of cogs and cables. Graghur leapt onto the platform and began to turn the wheel. The lift rose rapidly as he exerted his great strength. Kormak sprang forward onto the platform, but Graghur timed his counterstroke to perfection. The force of the blow sent Kormak spinning to the ground. The goblins swarmed forward, scratching, biting, stabbing.

Kormak rose to his feet, shrugging off his smaller attackers, ignoring his wounds. Graghur was still rising. The elevator platform was higher than Kormak's head now. He leapt once again, while Graghur's attention was on the wheel. The outstretched fingers of his left hand reached the bottom of the platform, gained purchase. He could not pull himself up one handed though and he did not want to let go of his blade. Having lost it once, he was not about to do so again.

Graghur brought one heavy, hob-nailed boot down on his fingers, Kormak dropped once more, falling atop a pile of goblins, lashing out and slicing them. Graghur's booming laughter rang out once more as he rose above the battle and out of Kormak's reach. Kormak cursed.

Something blazing passed overhead. An explosion sounded. Sasha had unleashed a runestone at the lift platform. The impact left it splintered and aflame but Graghur continued to rise, seemingly impervious to the flames. His mocking laughter echoed through the caves, then he looked up and noticed that the rope too was on fire.

A moment later it snapped, sending the whole blazing platform crashing back down towards the bottom of the cavern directly on top of Kormak. It descended like a meteor. Graghur howled with pain as the flames licked at his steadily blackening flesh. Kormak threw himself to one side as the platform impacted on the hard stone, sending sparks and splinters of burning wood flying everywhere.

The smoke almost choked him. The monstrous figure of the Goblin lord erupted from the flames, arms outstretched, claws flexed and ready to rend. His mouth was open wide. Madness filled his eyes, a sick determination to kill his tormentor if it was the last thing he did, apparent for all to see. He sprang at Kormak with the ferocity of a blood mad panther. The Guardian raised his sword and impaled the Old One on the dwarf-forged blade. The force of the impact drove him to his knees. Graghur's weight pushed down on him. Talons scrabbled against Kormak's armour. The Old One's tusks snapped closed inches from his throat. For a moment Kormak inhaled his foul breath and the stink of his burning flesh.

Graghur's scream rose above the clamour of battle, as he dissolved into a foul, black oil which caught fire and was consumed by the flame.

The sight of the death of their king demoralised the goblins. They turned to flee, leaving the small group of dwarves and humans standing amid a pile of corpses.

\*\*\*

Kormak raced over to where the bodies lay. One glance told him that Boreas was dead and Karnea was dying. The scholar lay there, very pale, eyes dimming.

"You get him?" she asked.

"Yes," Kormak said.

"I am glad," she said. "Get the Lost Rune back to Aethelas! Tell the tale of what happened here. Tell the dwarves of Aethelas about their kin."

"I will."

"Some good might come out of all this yet. The dwarves might yet be saved. More blades might be forged."

Kormak looked at the small band around him, thought about the numbers of dwarves left here. They were dying off and nothing was going to change that but he did not want to disappoint the dying woman. "I pray that you are right," he said. She was already far beyond hearing.

Ferik's heavy hand fell on his shoulder. In his other hand, he held Utti's head. "Come, we'd best get out of here before the goblins regroup. The monsters from the pits will keep them busy for a while longer. They are running out of control."

"I kept my part of the bargain," Kormak said, pointing to the outline of a body where Graghur had fallen.

"And we will keep ours," said Ferik. "You have the word of a dwarf on that. Without Graghur to lead them, we can take back the mine and reclaim the netherium."

In his heart, Kormak wondered at the truth of that, but right now he could not bring himself to care too much. He felt bad about abandoning Karnea and Boreas without burial. Still, there was something he needed to do. He reached down and unclamped the rune from the sorceress's arm and he picked up her sack.

"Come on," he said. "Let's get out of here."

\*\*\*

Kormak watched as the caravan prepared to leave Varigston. He felt better himself now he had a horse under him and a road out ahead.

There were a score of wagons all loaded with artefacts taken from the ruins of Khazduroth and there were armed men there to protect them. He looked down at Sasha. She adjusted little Tam's cloak, looked back and said something to her sister. The boy glanced at Kormak and smiled. He was glad that he had managed to keep one promise at least.

"You sure you won't come to Aethelas?" he said. He kept his voice low so no one could overhear him. "You had an agreement with Karnea. The rune was hers. You were to receive one quarter of its value. It could be worth a lot."

She smiled and spoke back just as softly, "And they might just decide to lock me up and keep what I know a secret. No, you were more than generous with Karnea's gold and letters of credit. We'll take the next caravan out and we'll quietly vanish once we hit some big city."

Kormak could not help but feel that might be the wiser course. Grand Master Darius might choose to be generous but then again, he might want the secret of the netherium kept safe for a few months longer. "As long as you keep your mouth shut, no one will come looking for you."

"You promise?" she said.

"I promise."

"What about you? Won't you have some explaining to do, with Karnea gone?"

"I have the rune and the promise of netherium. I am sure that will excuse a lot of failure on my part."

"I am sorry she died," Sasha said. "She was a nice woman even if she was a sorceress and she probably saved both our lives."

Kormak nodded and felt gloom settle on his shoulders like a weight. He looked at the mountains around him and back in the direction of the lost city. Clouds hung there, obscuring the sun.

A horn sounded, the wagons began to roll. He turned and waved farewell to the two women and the small boy and then they disappeared into the distance behind him.

## ABOUT THE AUTHOR

William King lives in Prague, Czech Republic with his lovely wife Radka and his sons Dan and William Karel. He has been a professional author and games developer for almost a quarter of a century. He is the creator of the bestselling Gotrek and Felix series for Black Library and the author of the World of Warcraft novel *Illidan*. Over a million copies of his books are in print in English. They have been translated into 8 languages.

He has been short-listed for the David Gemmell Legend Award. His short fiction has appeared in Year's Best SF and Best of Interzone. He has twice won the Origins Awards For Game Design. His hobbies include role-playing games and MMOs as well as travel.

His website can be found at: www.williamking.me

Word-of-mouth is crucial for any author to succeed. If you enjoyed the book, please consider leaving a review, even if it's only a line or two; it would make all the difference and would be very much appreciated.

Printed in Great Britain
by Amazon

56529127R00119